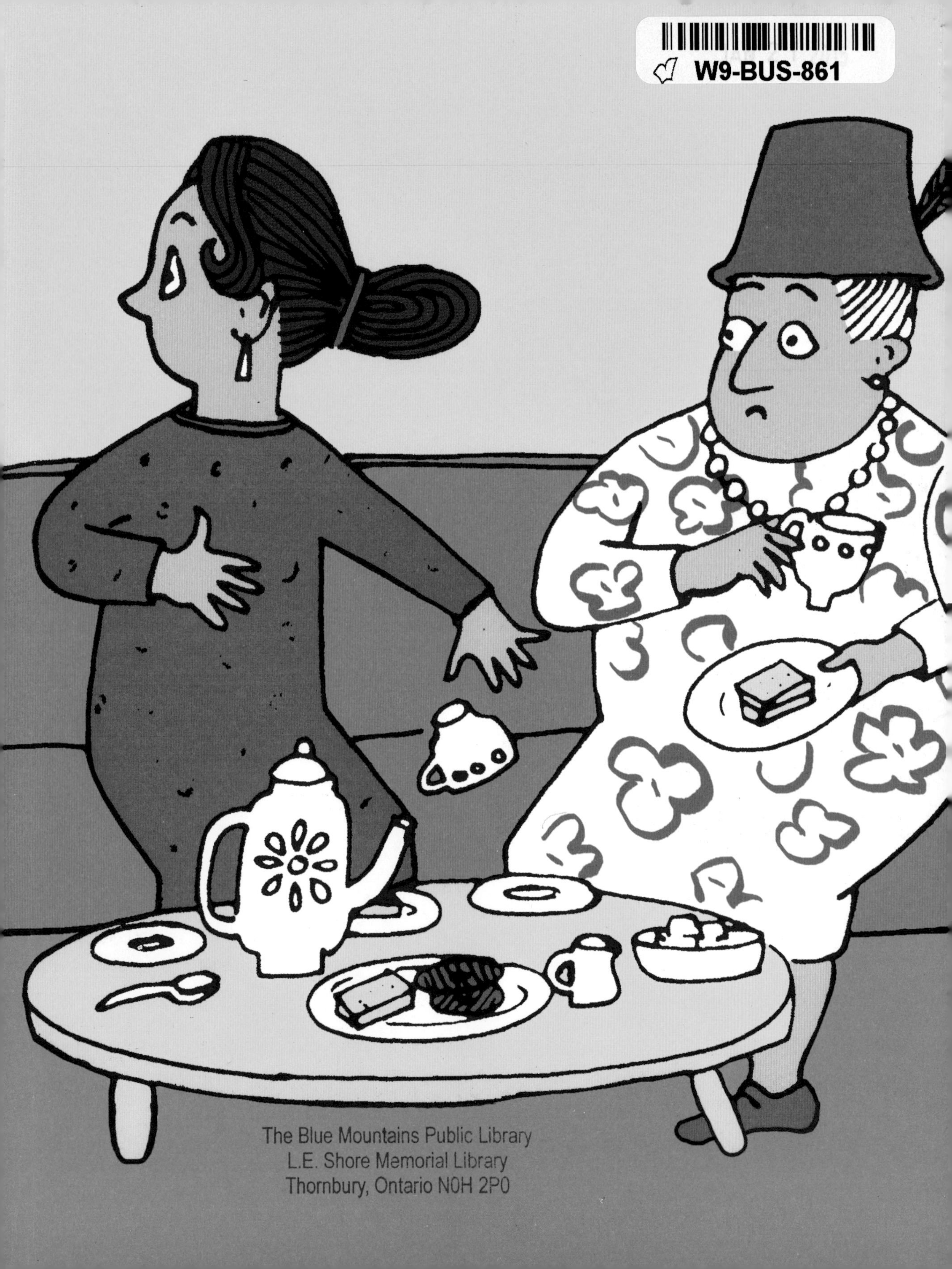

Text is © 1957, 1958, & 1959 by Astrid Lindgren, Saltkråkan AB. Illustrations are © 1957, 1958, & 1959 by Ingrid Vang Nyman, Saltkråkan AB. English translation is © 2013 by Tiina Nunnally. Illustrations are revised, restored, and colored by Björn Hedlund. Published by agreement with Rabén & Sjögren Agency. All rights reserved. No part of this book (except small portions for review purposes) may be reproduced in any form without written permission from Enfant or Rabén & Sjögren. Enfant is an imprint of Drawn & Quarterly. Originally published as *Pippi Ordnar Allt Och Andra Serier* in 2010 by Rabén & Sjögren (ISBN 978-91-29-67529-0). The translation of this book was funded by the Swedish Arts Council. Drawn & Quarterly; Post Office Box 48056; Montreal, Quebec; Canada; H2V 4S8; www.drawnandquarterly.com First hardcover edition: September 2013. Printed in Singapore. 10 9 8 7 6 5 4 3 2 1. Library and Archives Canada Cataloguing in Publication: Lindgren, Astrid, 1907–2002 [Pippi ordnar allt och andra serier. English]. Pippi Fixes Everything / by Astrid Lindgren & Ingrid Vang Nyman; translated by Tiina Nunnally. Translation of: Pippi ordnar allt och andra serier. 1. Graphic novels. I. Vang-Nyman, Ingrid, 1916–1959, artist II. Nunnally, Tiina, 1952–, translator III. Title. IV. Title: Pipi ordnar allt och andra serier. English. PZ7.7.L55Pif 2013 j741.5'9485 C2013-902358 5. Distributed in the USA by Farrar, Straus and Giroux; 18 West 18th St; New York, NY 10011; Orders: 888.330. 8477; Distributed in Canada by Raincoast Books; 2440 Viking Way; Vancouver, BC v6v 1n2; Orders: 800.663.5714. Distributed in the United Kingdom by Publishers Group U.K.; 63-66 Hatton Garden London; EC1N 8LE; info@pguk.co.uk

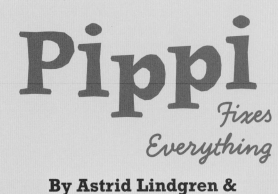

Pippi
Fixes
Everything

By Astrid Lindgren &
Ingrid Vang Nyman

Translated by Tiina Nunnally

ENFANT

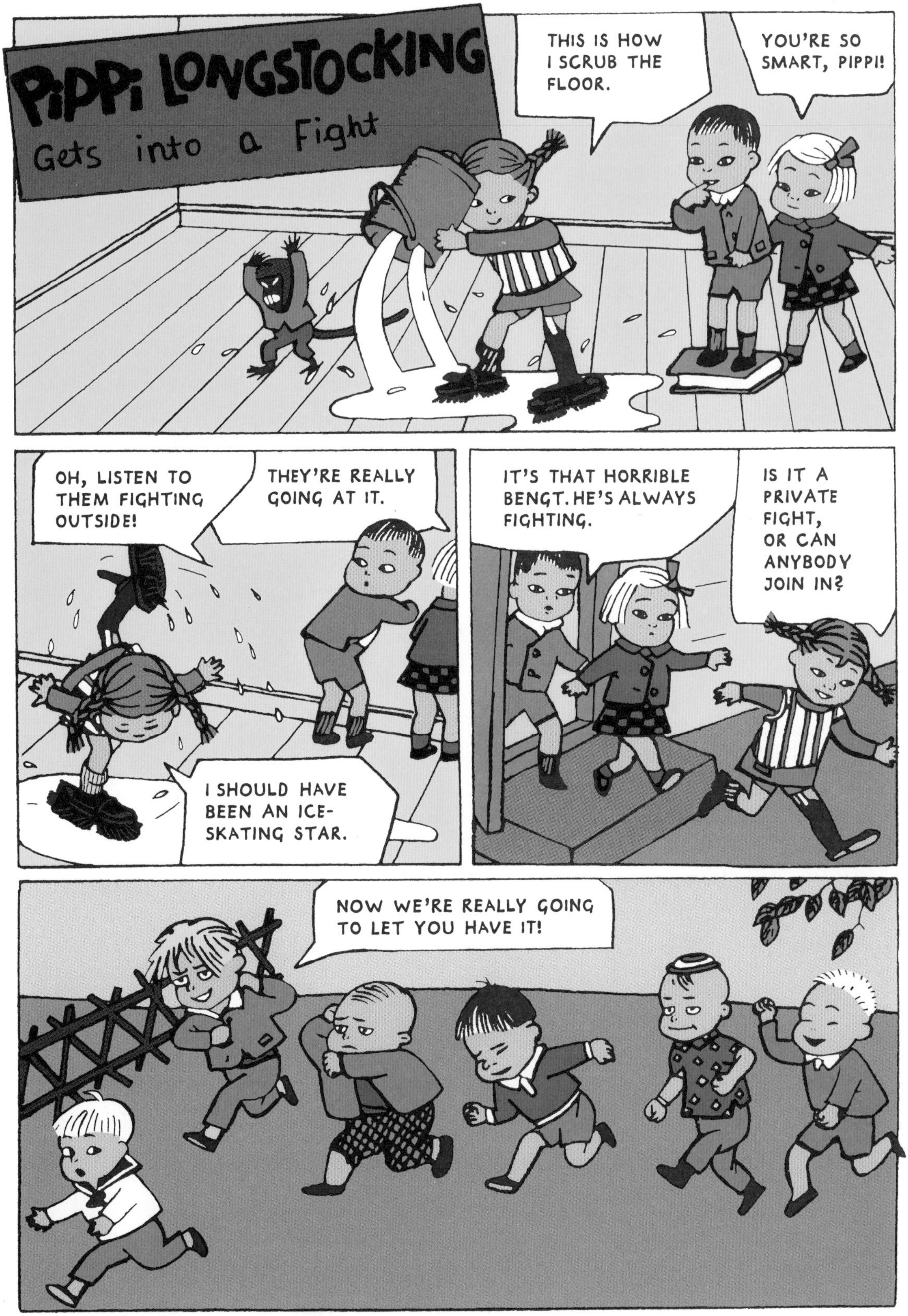
PIPPI LONGSTOCKING
Gets into a Fight
THIS IS HOW I SCRUB THE FLOOR.
YOU'RE SO SMART, PIPPI!
OH, LISTEN TO THEM FIGHTING OUTSIDE!
THEY'RE REALLY GOING AT IT.
I SHOULD HAVE BEEN AN ICE-SKATING STAR.
IT'S THAT HORRIBLE BENGT. HE'S ALWAYS FIGHTING.
IS IT A PRIVATE FIGHT, OR CAN ANYBODY JOIN IN?
NOW WE'RE REALLY GOING TO LET YOU HAVE IT!

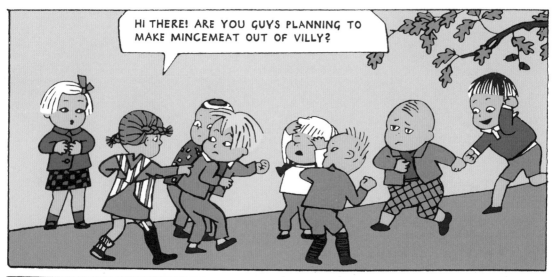

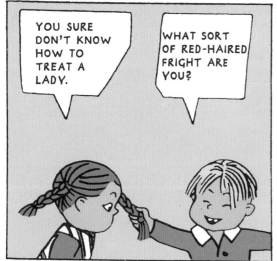

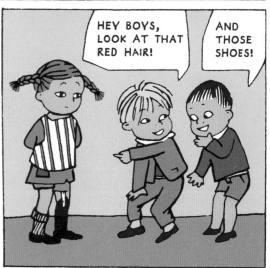

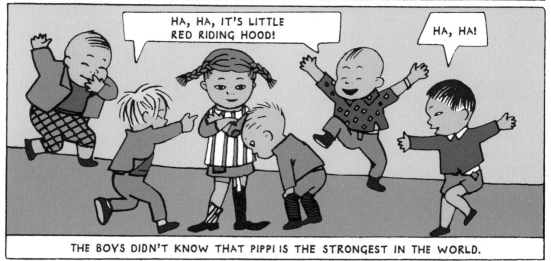

HI THERE! ARE YOU GUYS PLANNING TO MAKE MINCEMEAT OUT OF VILLY?
YOU SURE DON'T KNOW HOW TO TREAT A LADY.
WHAT SORT OF RED-HAIRED FRIGHT ARE YOU?
HEY BOYS, LOOK AT THAT RED HAIR!
AND THOSE SHOES!
HA, HA, IT'S LITTLE RED RIDING HOOD!
HA, HA!
THE BOYS DIDN'T KNOW THAT PIPPI IS THE STRONGEST IN THE WORLD.

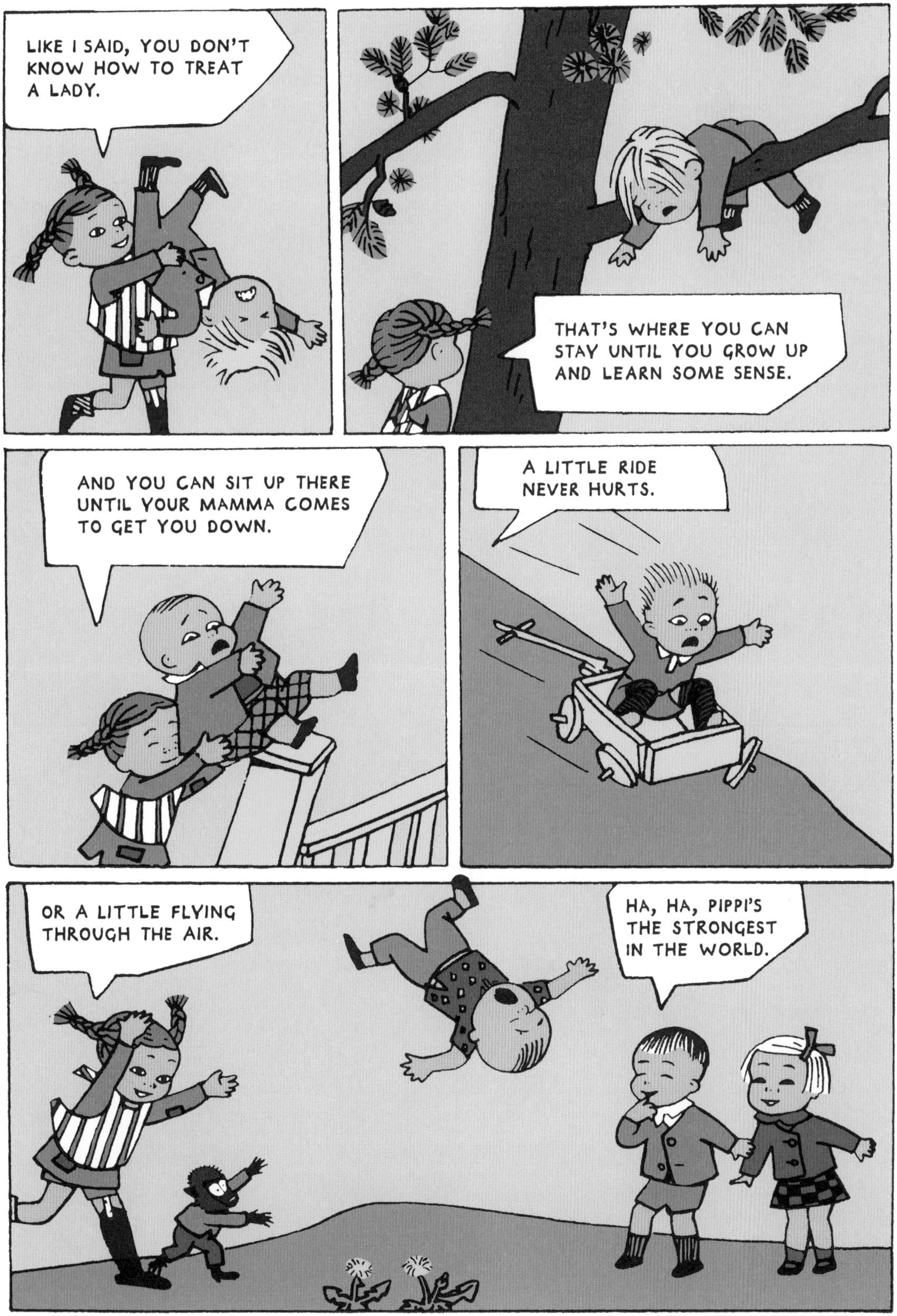
LIKE I SAID, YOU DON'T KNOW HOW TO TREAT A LADY.
THAT'S WHERE YOU CAN STAY UNTIL YOU GROW UP AND LEARN SOME SENSE.
AND YOU CAN SIT UP THERE UNTIL YOUR MAMMA COMES TO GET YOU DOWN.
A LITTLE RIDE NEVER HURTS.
OR A LITTLE FLYING THROUGH THE AIR.
HA, HA, PIPPI'S THE STRONGEST IN THE WORLD.

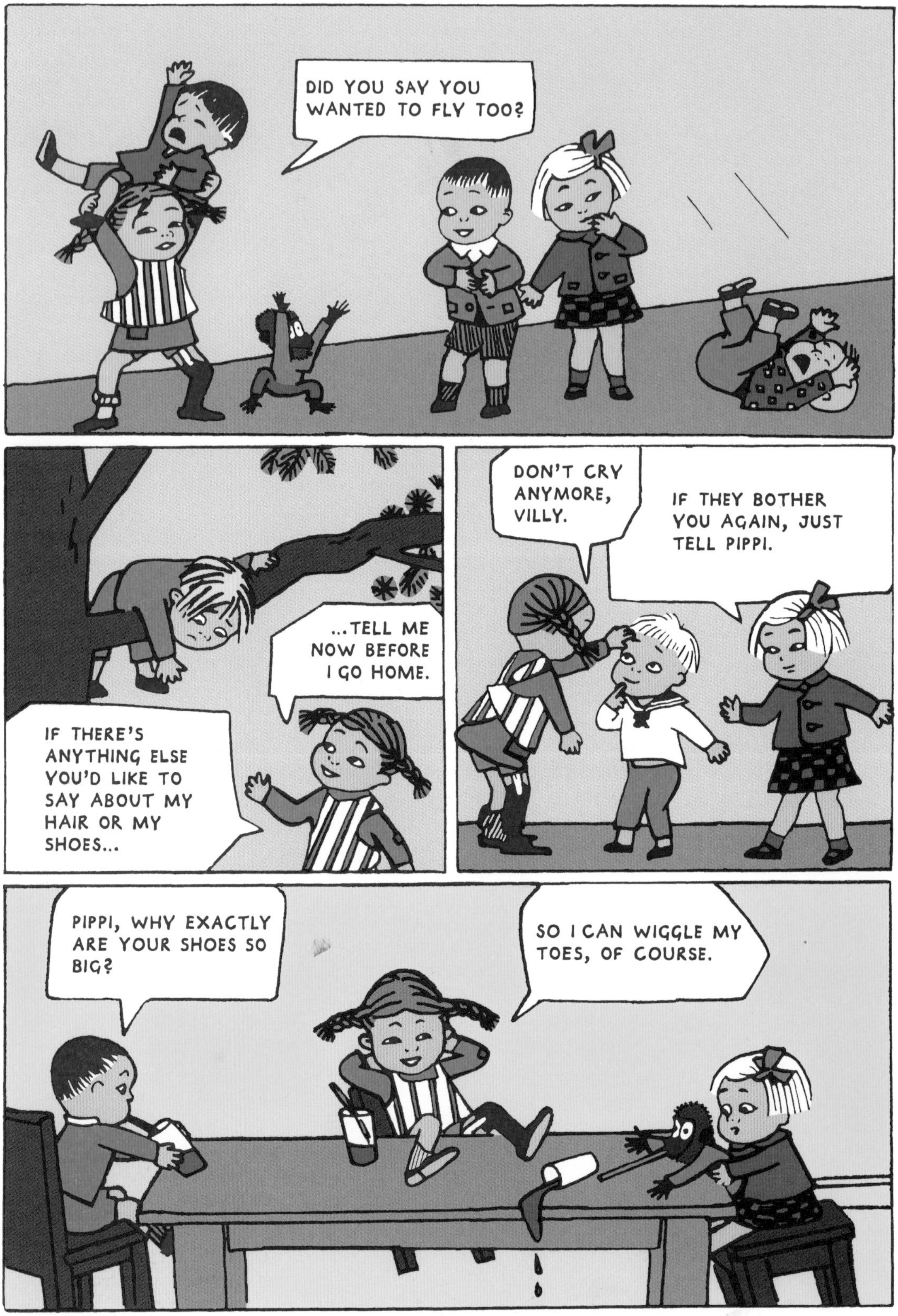
DID YOU SAY YOU WANTED TO FLY TOO?
IF THERE'S ANYTHING ELSE YOU'D LIKE TO SAY ABOUT MY HAIR OR MY SHOES...
...TELL ME NOW BEFORE I GO HOME.
DON'T CRY ANYMORE, VILLY.
IF THEY BOTHER YOU AGAIN, JUST TELL PIPPI.
PIPPI, WHY EXACTLY ARE YOUR SHOES SO BIG?
SO I CAN WIGGLE MY TOES, OF COURSE.

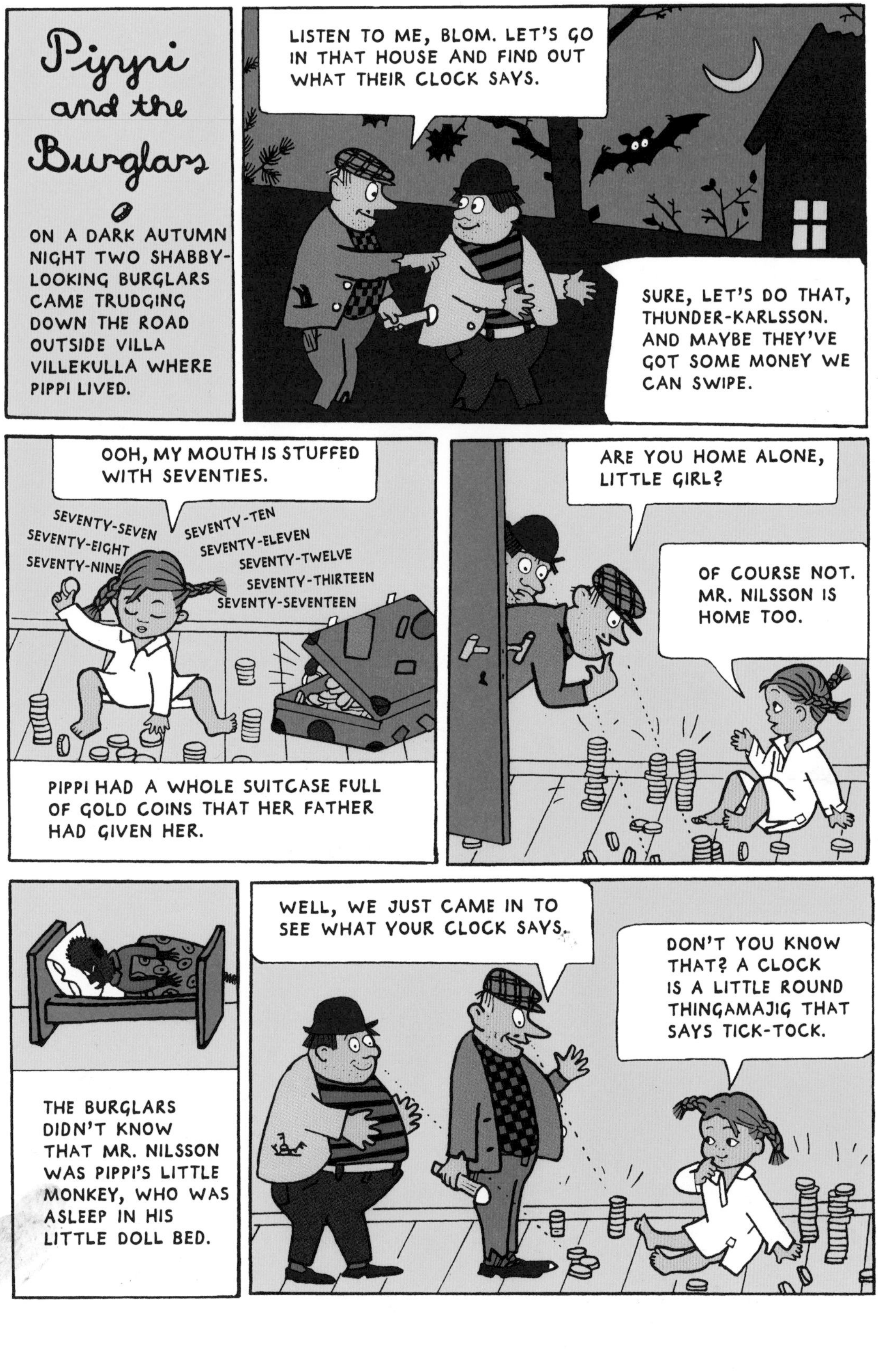

Pippi and the Burglars
ON A DARK AUTUMN NIGHT TWO SHABBY-LOOKING BURGLARS CAME TRUDGING DOWN THE ROAD OUTSIDE VILLA VILLEKULLA WHERE PIPPI LIVED.
LISTEN TO ME, BLOM. LET'S GO IN THAT HOUSE AND FIND OUT WHAT THEIR CLOCK SAYS.
SURE, LET'S DO THAT, THUNDER-KARLSSON. AND MAYBE THEY'VE GOT SOME MONEY WE CAN SWIPE.
OOH, MY MOUTH IS STUFFED WITH SEVENTIES.
SEVENTY-SEVEN
SEVENTY-EIGHT
SEVENTY-NINE
SEVENTY-TEN
SEVENTY-ELEVEN
SEVENTY-TWELVE
SEVENTY-THIRTEEN
SEVENTY-SEVENTEEN
PIPPI HAD A WHOLE SUITCASE FULL OF GOLD COINS THAT HER FATHER HAD GIVEN HER.
ARE YOU HOME ALONE, LITTLE GIRL?
OF COURSE NOT. MR. NILSSON IS HOME TOO.
THE BURGLARS DIDN'T KNOW THAT MR. NILSSON WAS PIPPI'S LITTLE MONKEY, WHO WAS ASLEEP IN HIS LITTLE DOLL BED.
WELL, WE JUST CAME IN TO SEE WHAT YOUR CLOCK SAYS.
DON'T YOU KNOW THAT? A CLOCK IS A LITTLE ROUND THINGAMAJIG THAT SAYS TICK-TOCK.

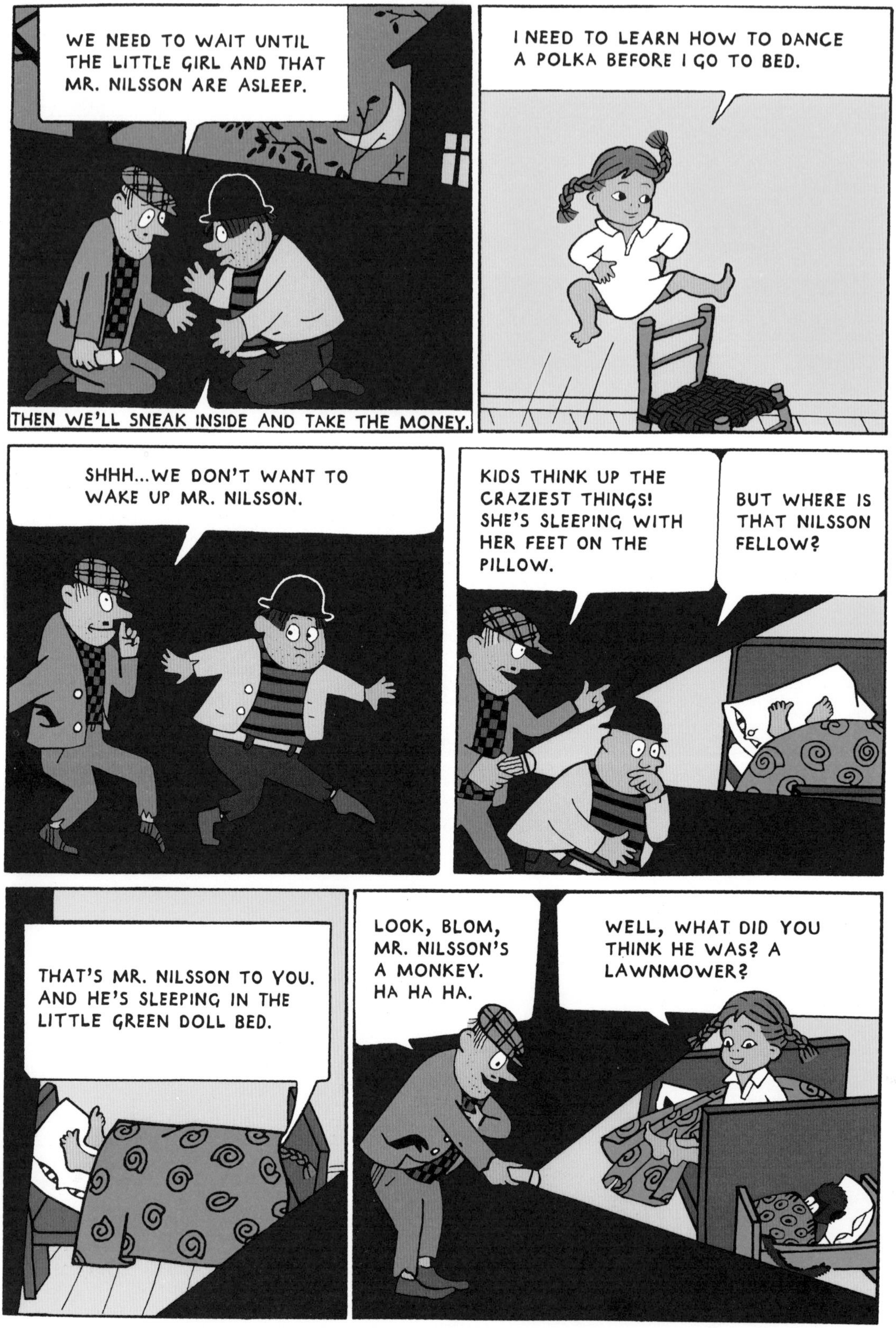
WE NEED TO WAIT UNTIL THE LITTLE GIRL AND THAT MR. NILSSON ARE ASLEEP.
THEN WE'LL SNEAK INSIDE AND TAKE THE MONEY.
I NEED TO LEARN HOW TO DANCE A POLKA BEFORE I GO TO BED.
SHHH...WE DON'T WANT TO WAKE UP MR. NILSSON.
KIDS THINK UP THE CRAZIEST THINGS! SHE'S SLEEPING WITH HER FEET ON THE PILLOW.
BUT WHERE IS THAT NILSSON FELLOW?
THAT'S MR. NILSSON TO YOU. AND HE'S SLEEPING IN THE LITTLE GREEN DOLL BED.
LOOK, BLOM, MR. NILSSON'S A MONKEY. HA HA HA.
WELL, WHAT DID YOU THINK HE WAS? A LAWNMOWER?

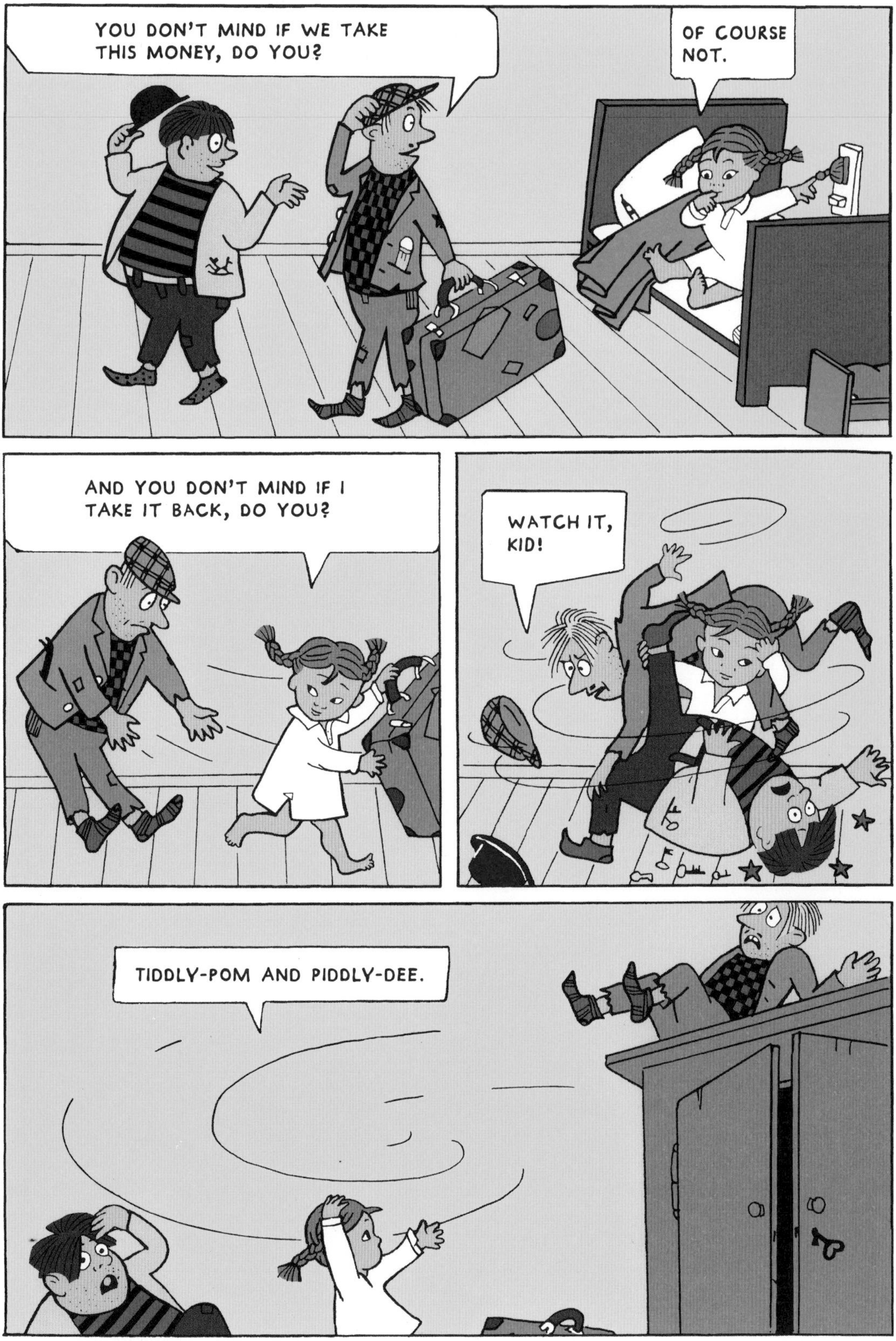
YOU DON'T MIND IF WE TAKE THIS MONEY, DO YOU?
OF COURSE NOT.
AND YOU DON'T MIND IF I TAKE IT BACK, DO YOU?
WATCH IT, KID!
TIDDLY-POM AND PIDDLY-DEE.

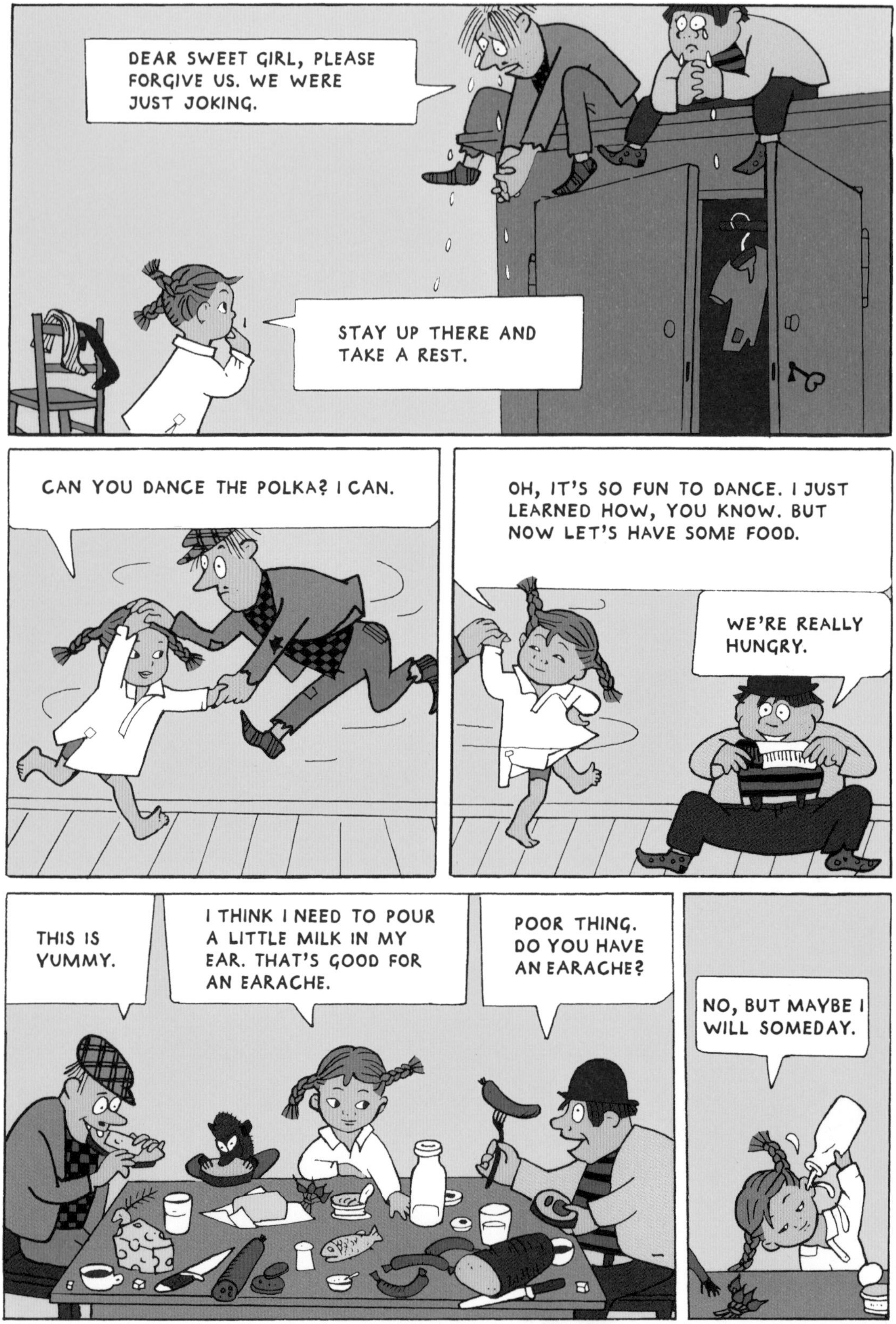
DEAR SWEET GIRL, PLEASE FORGIVE US. WE WERE JUST JOKING.
STAY UP THERE AND TAKE A REST.
CAN YOU DANCE THE POLKA? I CAN.
OH, IT'S SO FUN TO DANCE. I JUST LEARNED HOW, YOU KNOW. BUT NOW LET'S HAVE SOME FOOD.
WE'RE REALLY HUNGRY.
THIS IS YUMMY.
I THINK I NEED TO POUR A LITTLE MILK IN MY EAR. THAT'S GOOD FOR AN EARACHE.
POOR THING. DO YOU HAVE AN EARACHE?
NO, BUT MAYBE I WILL SOMEDAY.

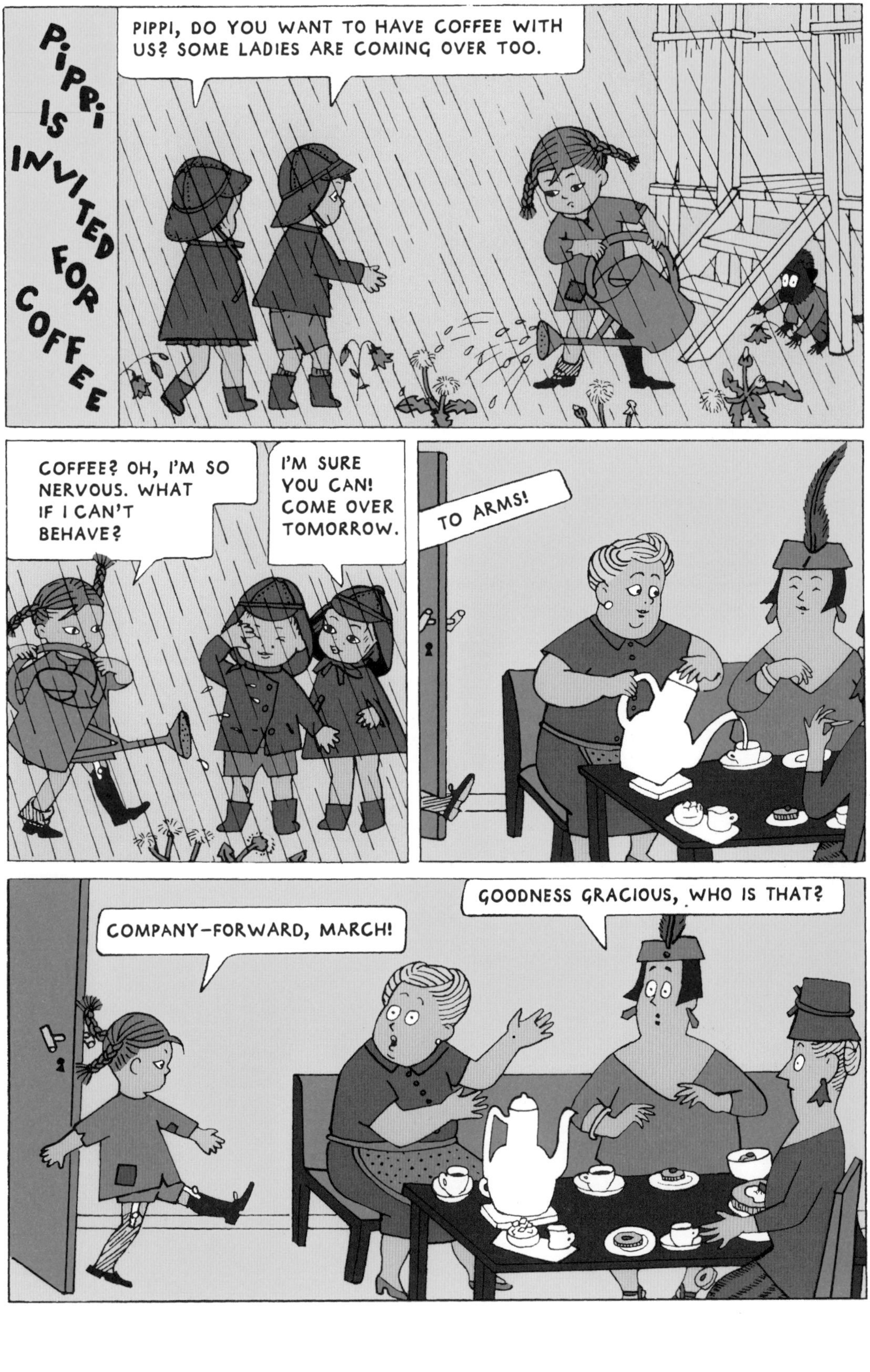

PIPPI IS INVITED FOR COFFEE
PIPPI, DO YOU WANT TO HAVE COFFEE WITH US? SOME LADIES ARE COMING OVER TOO.
COFFEE? OH, I'M SO NERVOUS. WHAT IF I CAN'T BEHAVE?
I'M SURE YOU CAN! COME OVER TOMORROW.
TO ARMS!
COMPANY—FORWARD, MARCH!
GOODNESS GRACIOUS, WHO IS THAT?

ARMS, FORWARD. KNEES, BEND! I'M A LITTLE SHY, YOU SEE, SO I NEED TO ISSUE ORDERS.

LITTLE CHILDREN SHOULD BE SEEN AND NOT HEARD.

WHY'S THAT? THE EARS NEED A LITTLE EXERCISE, TOO. THEY'RE NOT JUST FOR WIGGLING, ARE THEY?

OH, WHAT CHARMING LADIES!

PIPPI, COME AND SIT OVER HERE SO WE CAN SHOW YOU THE ALBUM.

SURE, BUT FIRST I NEED SOMETHING IN MY BELLY.

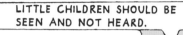

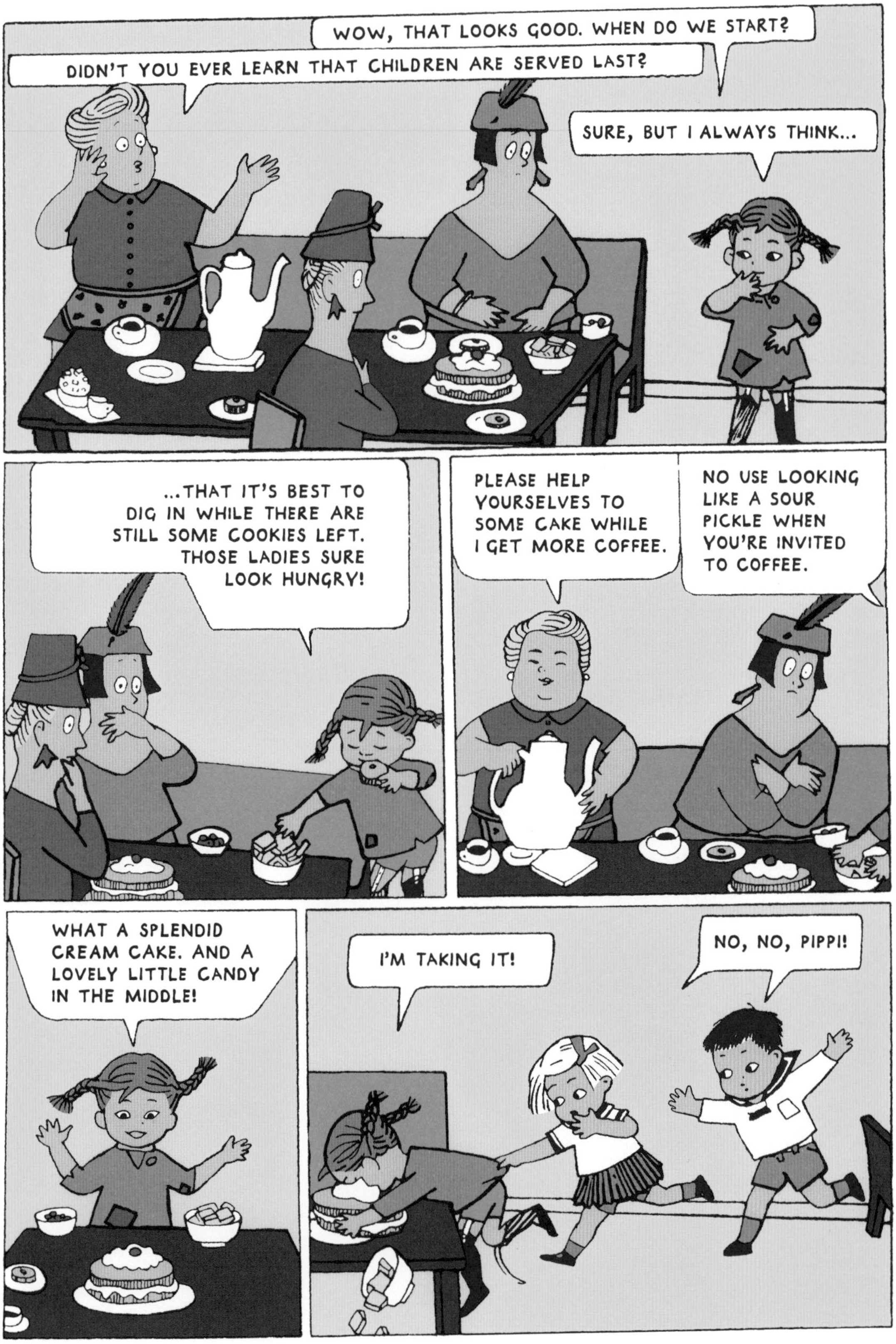

WOW, THAT LOOKS GOOD. WHEN DO WE START?
DIDN'T YOU EVER LEARN THAT CHILDREN ARE SERVED LAST?
SURE, BUT I ALWAYS THINK...
...THAT IT'S BEST TO DIG IN WHILE THERE ARE STILL SOME COOKIES LEFT. THOSE LADIES SURE LOOK HUNGRY!
PLEASE HELP YOURSELVES TO SOME CAKE WHILE I GET MORE COFFEE.
NO USE LOOKING LIKE A SOUR PICKLE WHEN YOU'RE INVITED TO COFFEE.
WHAT A SPLENDID CREAM CAKE. AND A LOVELY LITTLE CANDY IN THE MIDDLE!
I'M TAKING IT!
NO, NO, PIPPI!

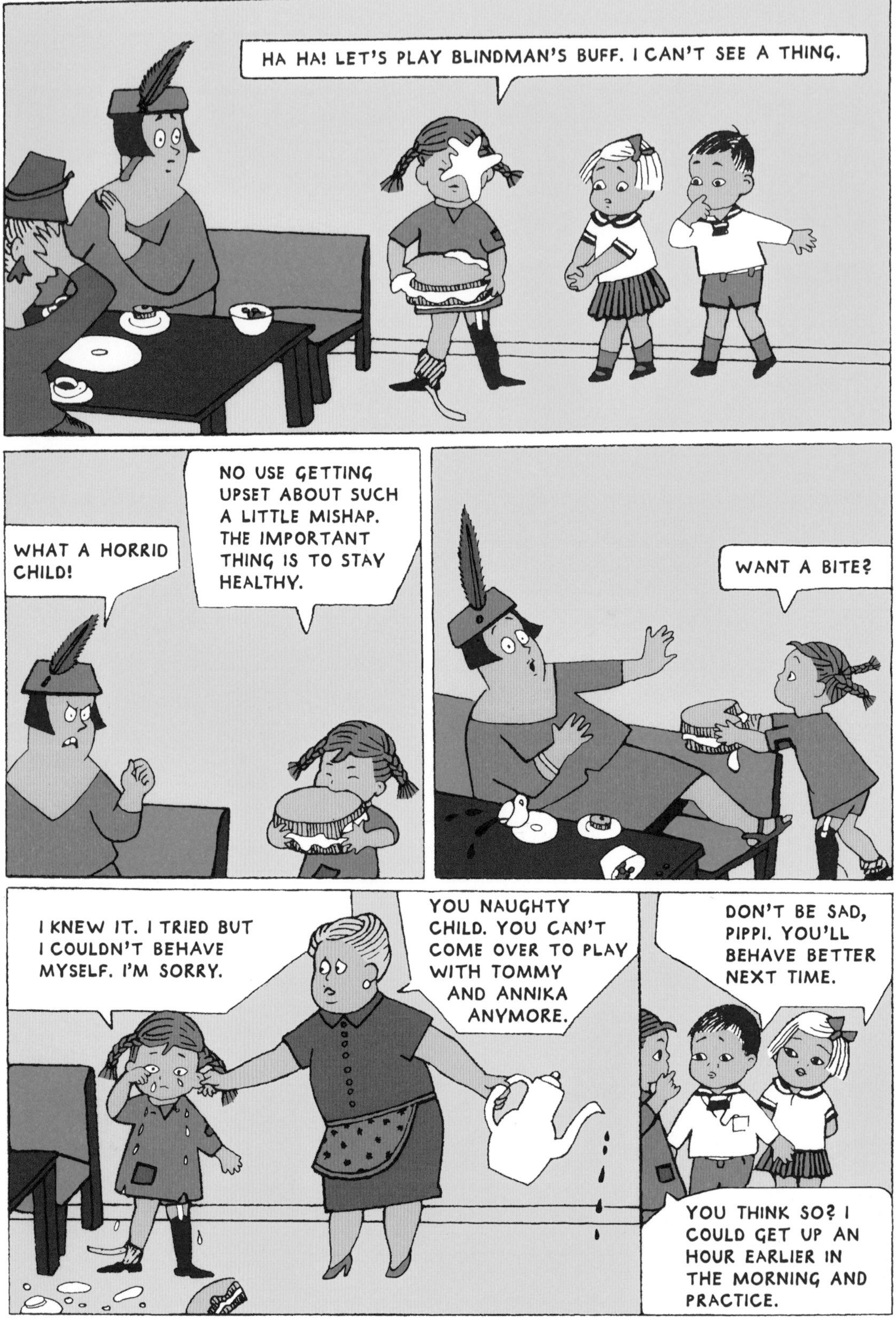
HA HA! LET'S PLAY BLINDMAN'S BUFF. I CAN'T SEE A THING.
WHAT A HORRID CHILD!
NO USE GETTING UPSET ABOUT SUCH A LITTLE MISHAP. THE IMPORTANT THING IS TO STAY HEALTHY.
WANT A BITE?
I KNEW IT. I TRIED BUT I COULDN'T BEHAVE MYSELF. I'M SORRY.
YOU NAUGHTY CHILD. YOU CAN'T COME OVER TO PLAY WITH TOMMY AND ANNIKA ANYMORE.
DON'T BE SAD, PIPPI. YOU'LL BEHAVE BETTER NEXT TIME.
YOU THINK SO? I COULD GET UP AN HOUR EARLIER IN THE MORNING AND PRACTICE.

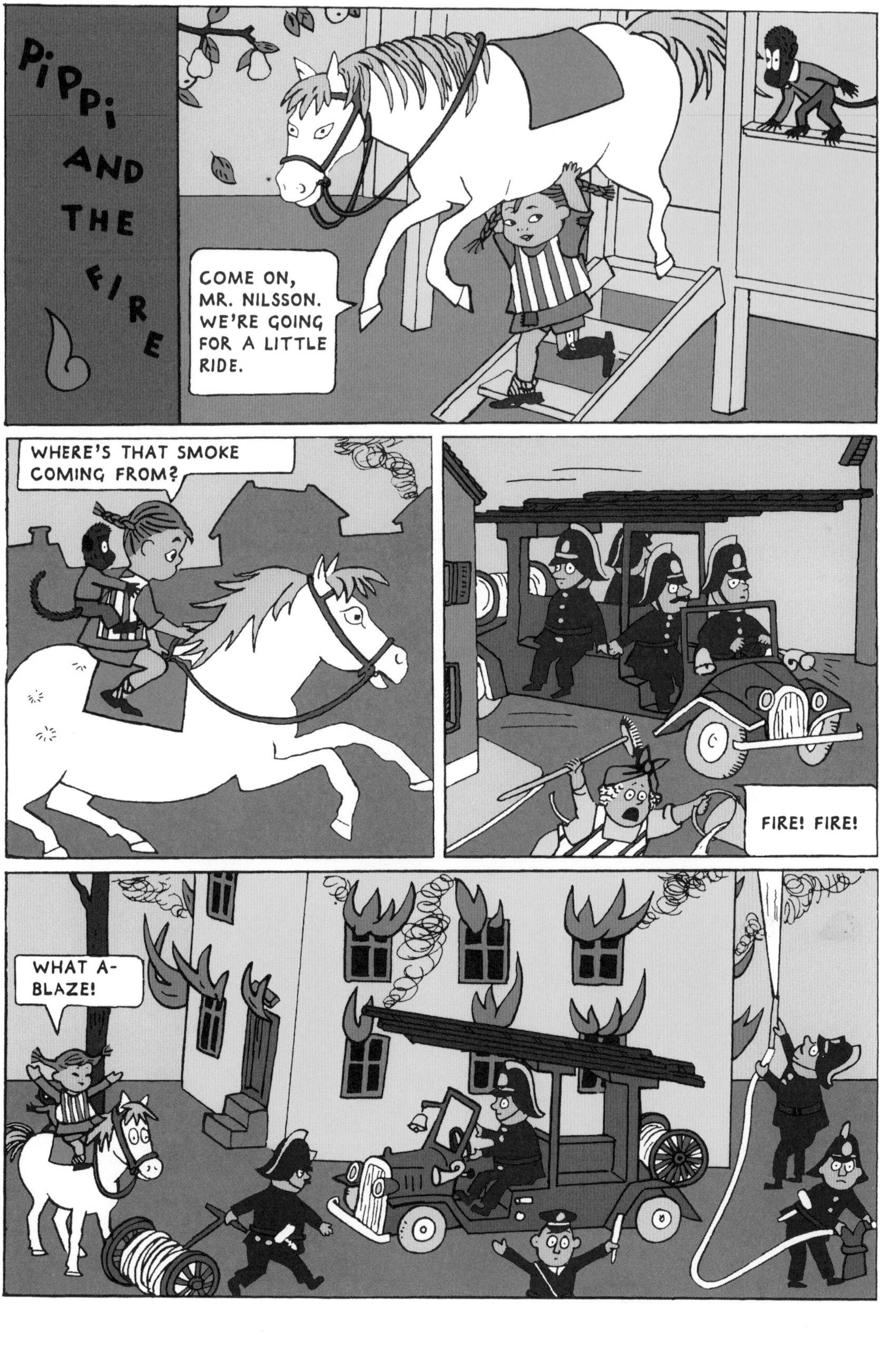
PIPPI AND THE FIRE
COME ON, MR. NILSSON. WE'RE GOING FOR A LITTLE RIDE.
WHERE'S THAT SMOKE COMING FROM?
FIRE! FIRE!
WHAT A-BLAZE!

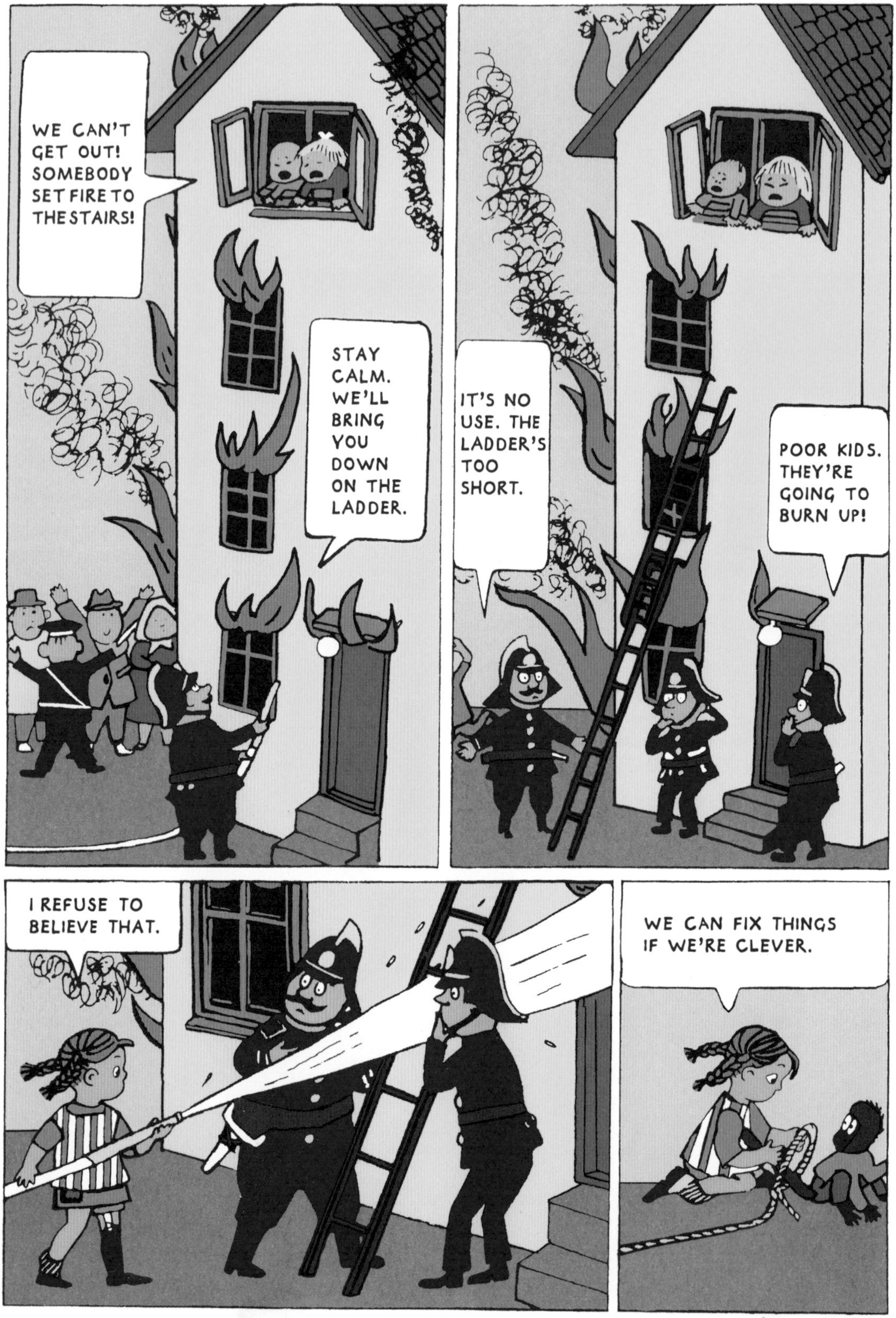
WE CAN'T GET OUT! SOMEBODY SET FIRE TO THE STAIRS!
STAY CALM. WE'LL BRING YOU DOWN ON THE LADDER.
IT'S NO USE. THE LADDER'S TOO SHORT.
POOR KIDS. THEY'RE GOING TO BURN UP!
I REFUSE TO BELIEVE THAT.
WE CAN FIX THINGS IF WE'RE CLEVER.

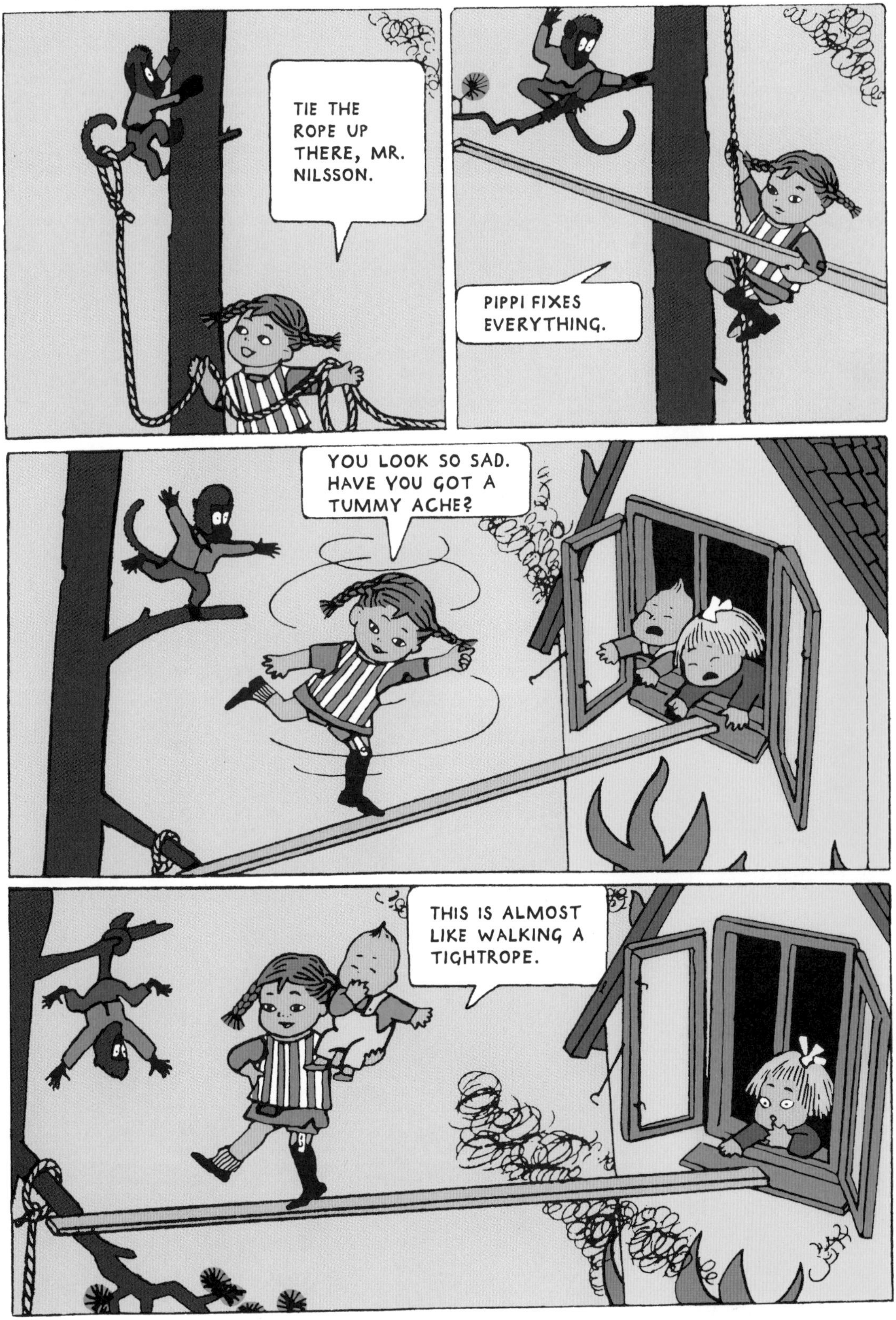

TIE THE ROPE UP THERE, MR. NILSSON.
PIPPI FIXES EVERYTHING.
YOU LOOK SO SAD. HAVE YOU GOT A TUMMY ACHE?
THIS IS ALMOST LIKE WALKING A TIGHTROPE.

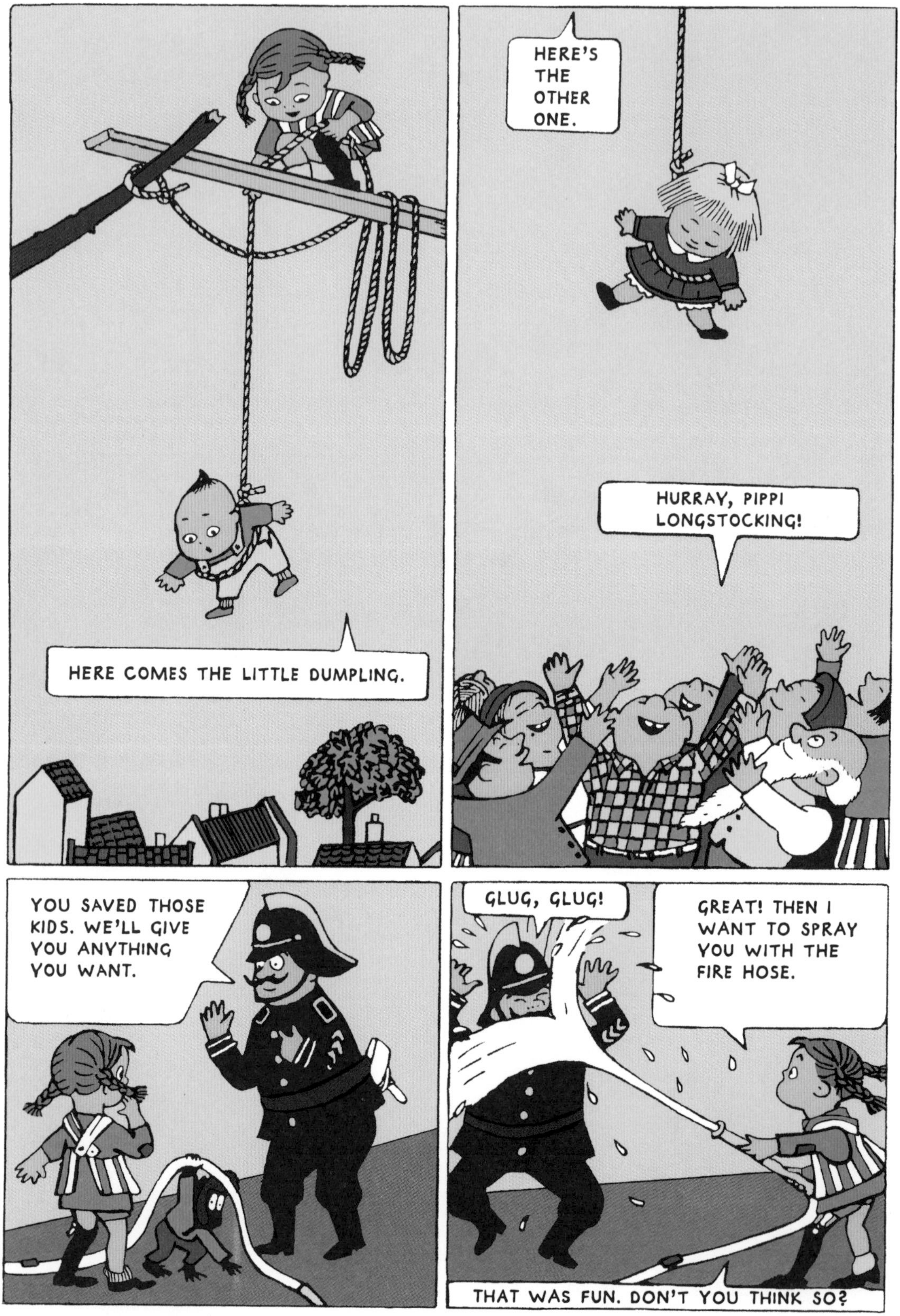
HERE COMES THE LITTLE DUMPLING.
HERE'S THE OTHER ONE.
HURRAY, PIPPI LONGSTOCKING!
YOU SAVED THOSE KIDS. WE'LL GIVE YOU ANYTHING YOU WANT.
GREAT! THEN I WANT TO SPRAY YOU WITH THE FIRE HOSE.
GLUG, GLUG!
THAT WAS FUN. DON'T YOU THINK SO?

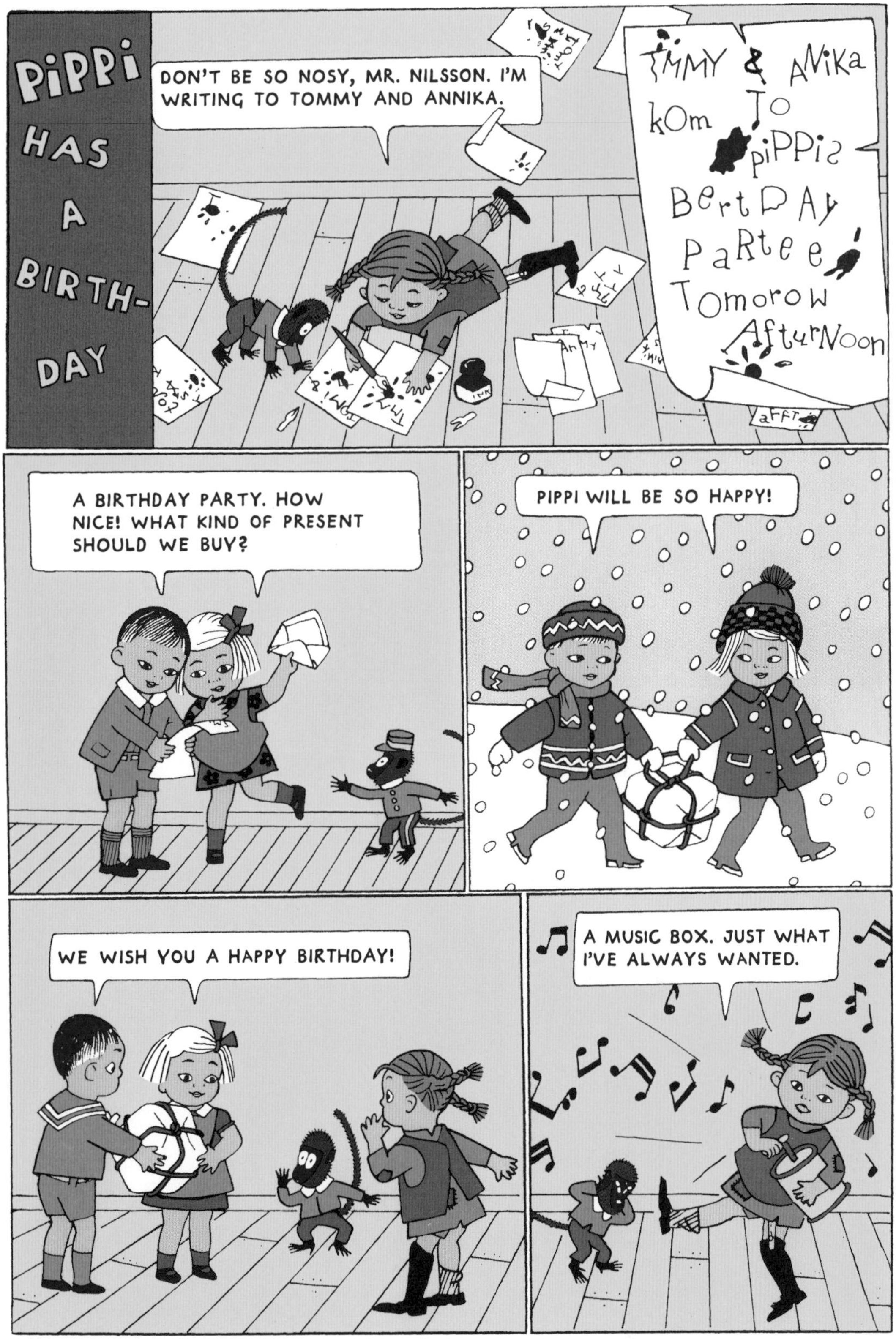
PIPPI HAS A BIRTH-DAY
DON'T BE SO NOSY, MR. NILSSON. I'M WRITING TO TOMMY AND ANNIKA.
TMMY & ANIKA kOm To piPPis BertDAy PaRtee Tomorow AfturNoon
A BIRTHDAY PARTY. HOW NICE! WHAT KIND OF PRESENT SHOULD WE BUY?
PIPPI WILL BE SO HAPPY!
WE WISH YOU A HAPPY BIRTHDAY!
A MUSIC BOX. JUST WHAT I'VE ALWAYS WANTED.

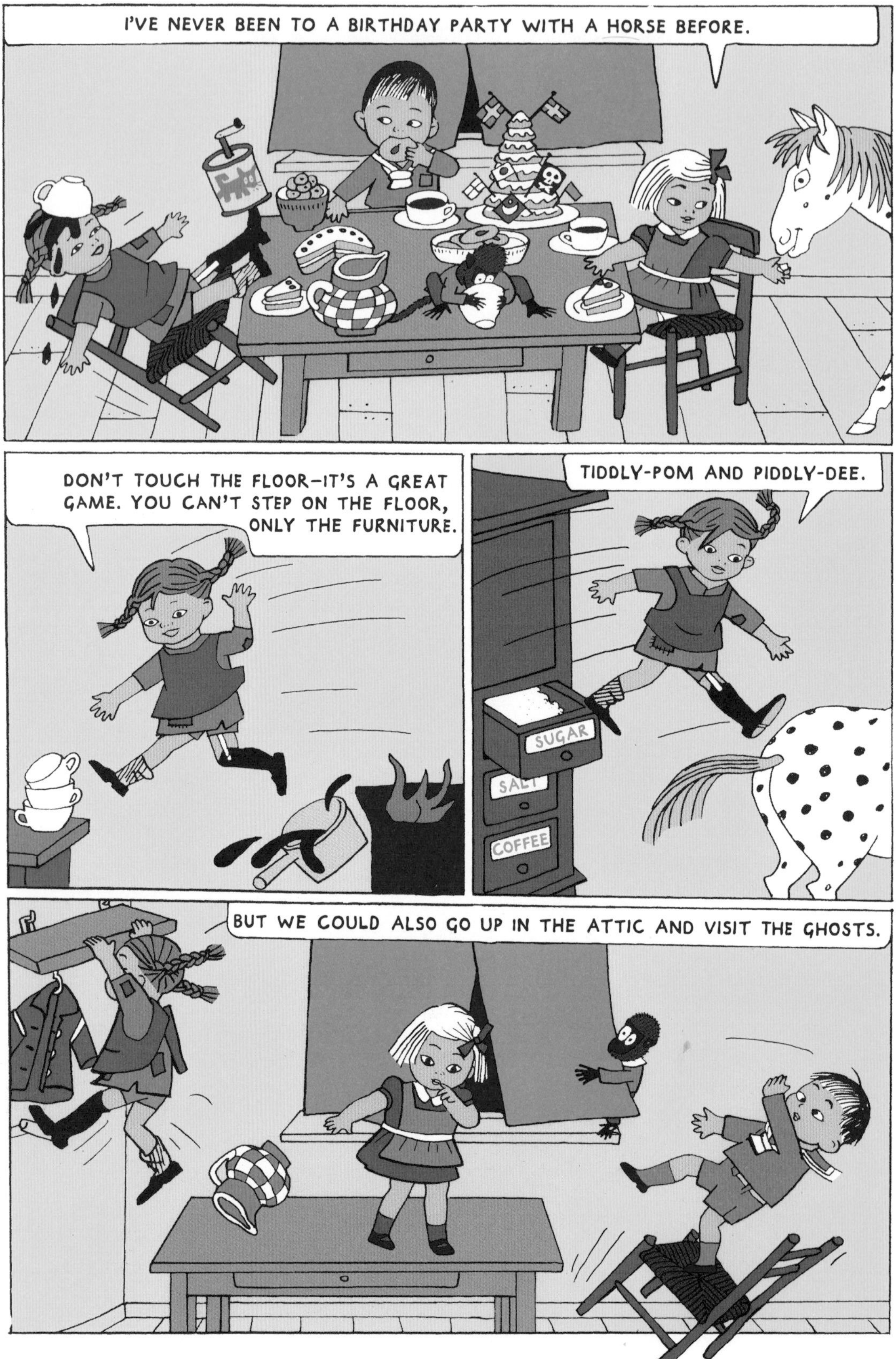
I'VE NEVER BEEN TO A BIRTHDAY PARTY WITH A HORSE BEFORE.
DON'T TOUCH THE FLOOR—IT'S A GREAT GAME. YOU CAN'T STEP ON THE FLOOR, ONLY THE FURNITURE.
TIDDLY-POM AND PIDDLY-DEE.
SUGAR
SALT
COFFEE
BUT WE COULD ALSO GO UP IN THE ATTIC AND VISIT THE GHOSTS.

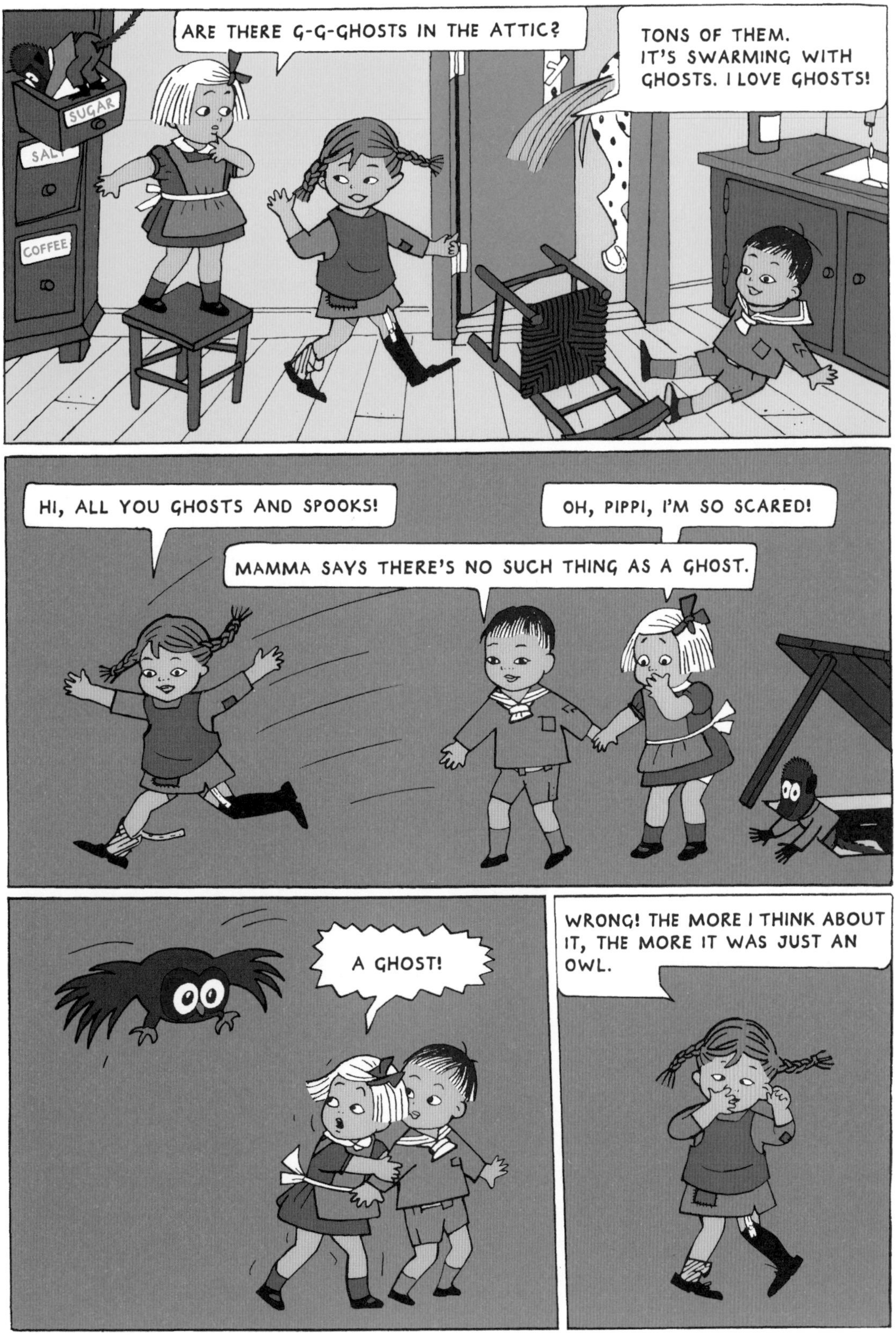
ARE THERE G-G-GHOSTS IN THE ATTIC?
TONS OF THEM. IT'S SWARMING WITH GHOSTS. I LOVE GHOSTS!
SUGAR
SALT
COFFEE
HI, ALL YOU GHOSTS AND SPOOKS!
OH, PIPPI, I'M SO SCARED!
MAMMA SAYS THERE'S NO SUCH THING AS A GHOST.
A GHOST!
WRONG! THE MORE I THINK ABOUT IT, THE MORE IT WAS JUST AN OWL.

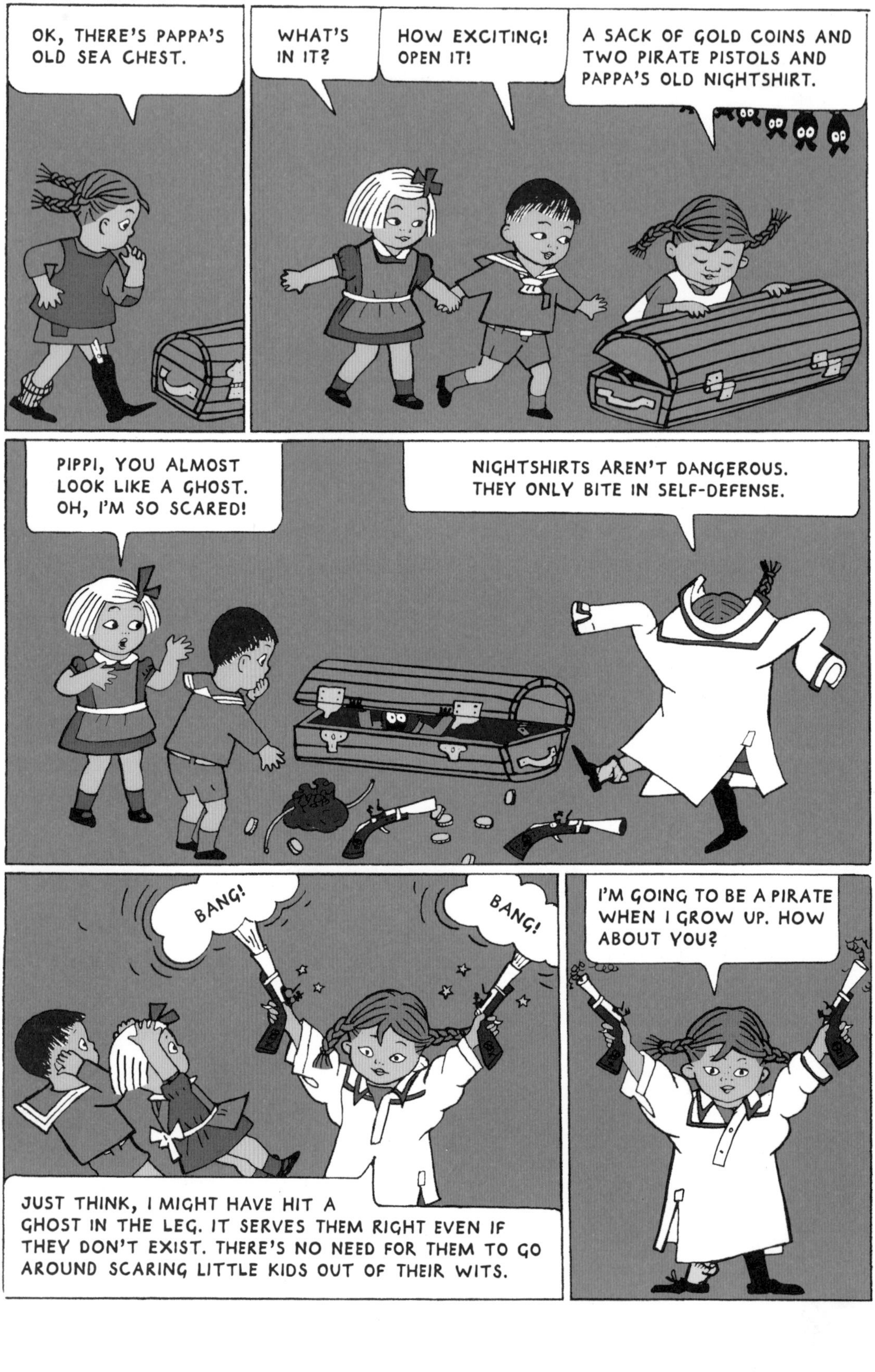
OK, THERE'S PAPPA'S OLD SEA CHEST.
WHAT'S IN IT?
HOW EXCITING! OPEN IT!
A SACK OF GOLD COINS AND TWO PIRATE PISTOLS AND PAPPA'S OLD NIGHTSHIRT.
PIPPI, YOU ALMOST LOOK LIKE A GHOST. OH, I'M SO SCARED!
NIGHTSHIRTS AREN'T DANGEROUS. THEY ONLY BITE IN SELF-DEFENSE.
BANG!
BANG!
JUST THINK, I MIGHT HAVE HIT A GHOST IN THE LEG. IT SERVES THEM RIGHT EVEN IF THEY DON'T EXIST. THERE'S NO NEED FOR THEM TO GO AROUND SCARING LITTLE KIDS OUT OF THEIR WITS.
I'M GOING TO BE A PIRATE WHEN I GROW UP. HOW ABOUT YOU?

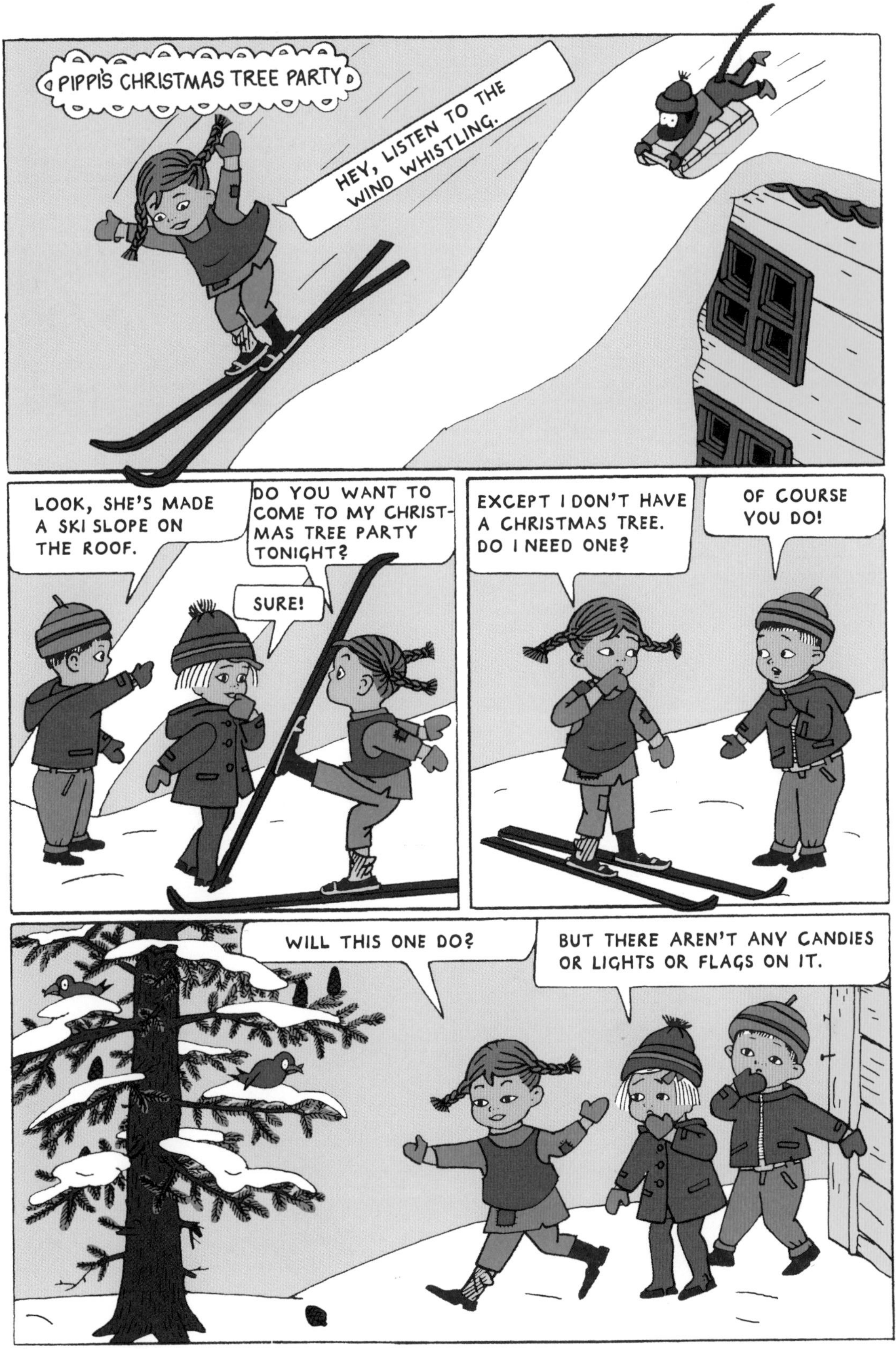
PIPPI'S CHRISTMAS TREE PARTY
HEY, LISTEN TO THE WIND WHISTLING.
LOOK, SHE'S MADE A SKI SLOPE ON THE ROOF.
DO YOU WANT TO COME TO MY CHRIST-MAS TREE PARTY TONIGHT?
SURE!
EXCEPT I DON'T HAVE A CHRISTMAS TREE. DO I NEED ONE?
OF COURSE YOU DO!
WILL THIS ONE DO?
BUT THERE AREN'T ANY CANDIES OR LIGHTS OR FLAGS ON IT.

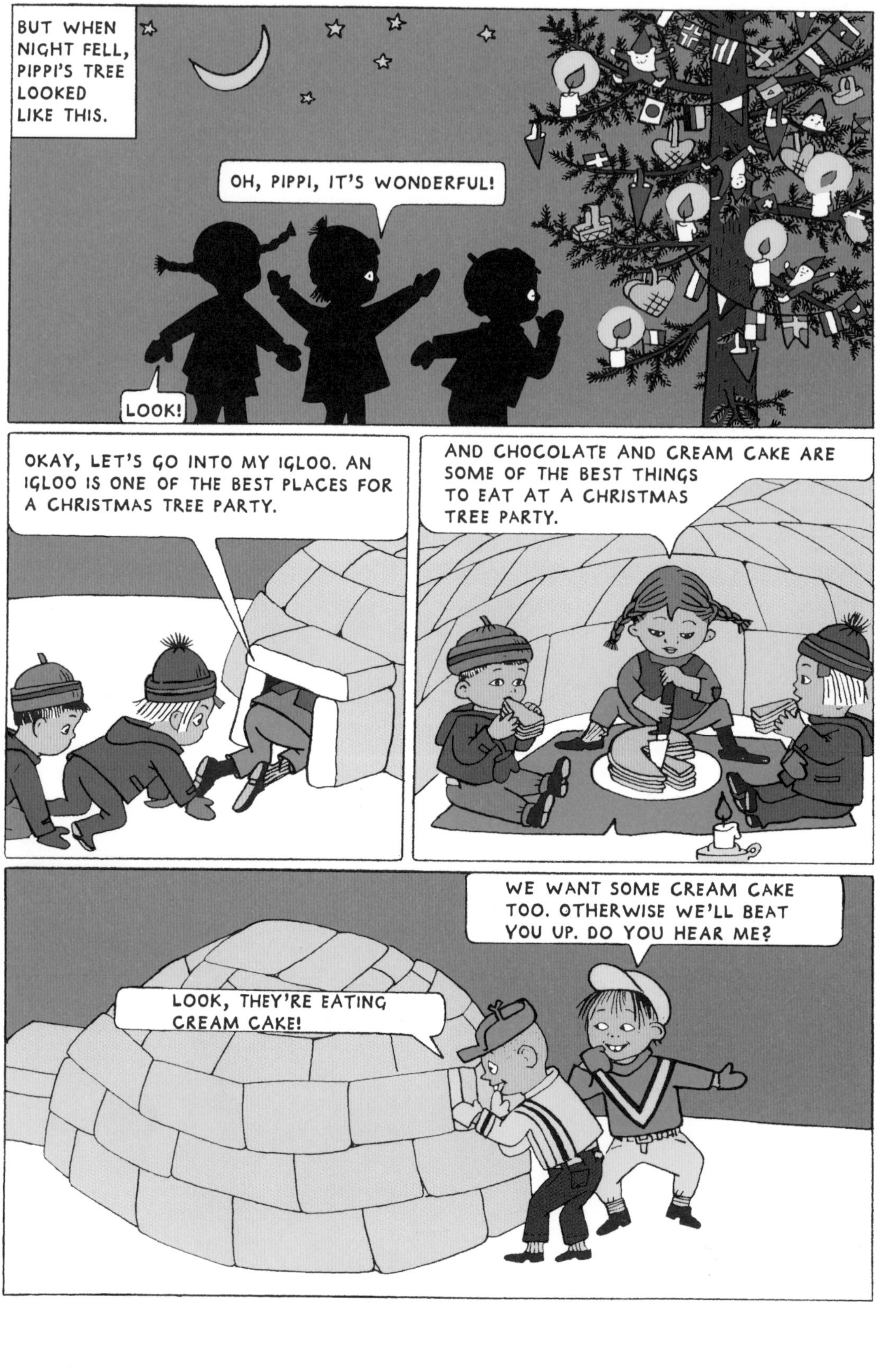
BUT WHEN NIGHT FELL, PIPPI'S TREE LOOKED LIKE THIS.
OH, PIPPI, IT'S WONDERFUL!
LOOK!
OKAY, LET'S GO INTO MY IGLOO. AN IGLOO IS ONE OF THE BEST PLACES FOR A CHRISTMAS TREE PARTY.
AND CHOCOLATE AND CREAM CAKE ARE SOME OF THE BEST THINGS TO EAT AT A CHRISTMAS TREE PARTY.
WE WANT SOME CREAM CAKE TOO. OTHERWISE WE'LL BEAT YOU UP. DO YOU HEAR ME?
LOOK, THEY'RE EATING CREAM CAKE!

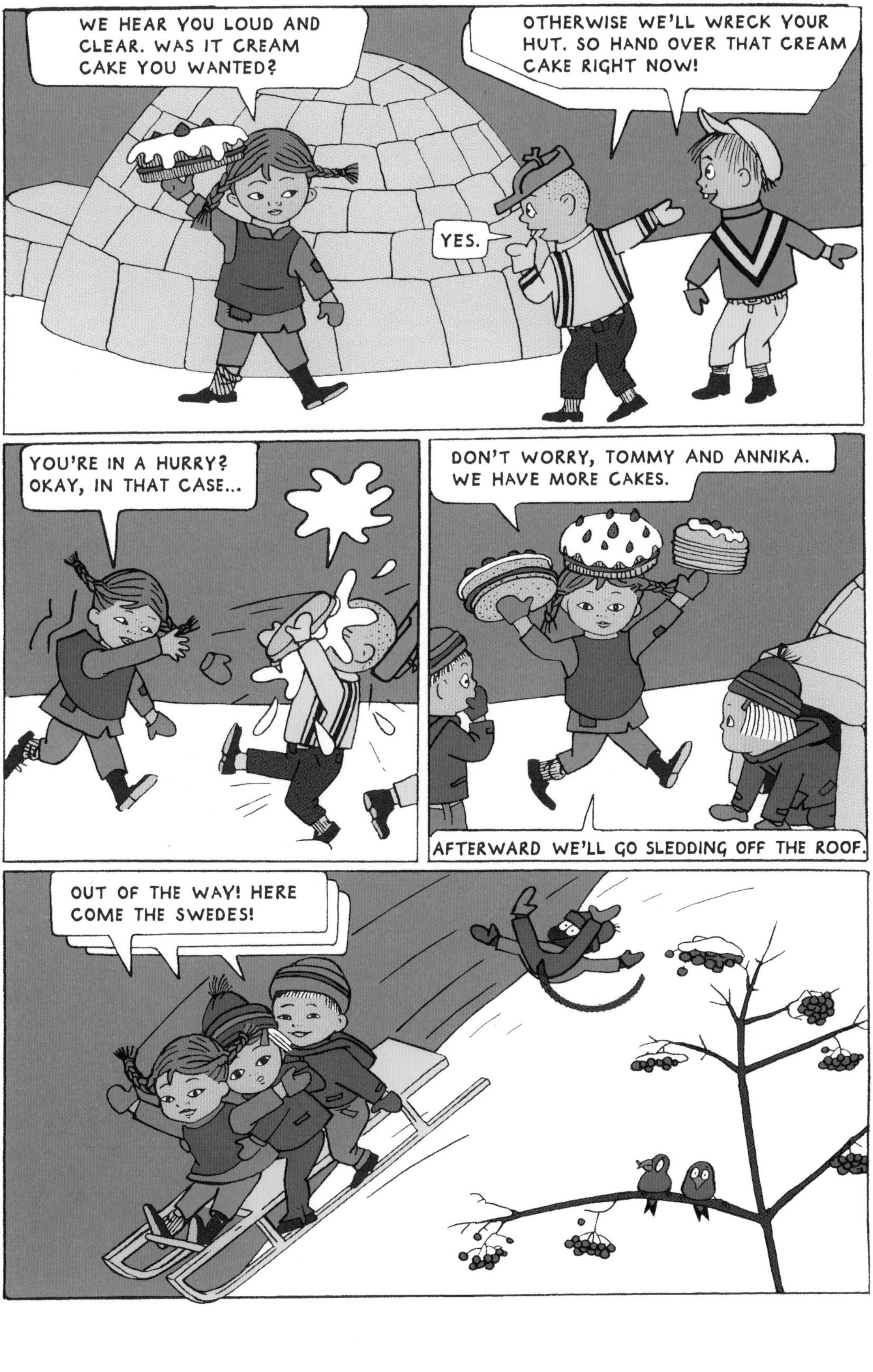
WE HEAR YOU LOUD AND CLEAR. WAS IT CREAM CAKE YOU WANTED?
OTHERWISE WE'LL WRECK YOUR HUT. SO HAND OVER THAT CREAM CAKE RIGHT NOW!
YES.
YOU'RE IN A HURRY? OKAY, IN THAT CASE...
DON'T WORRY, TOMMY AND ANNIKA. WE HAVE MORE CAKES.
AFTERWARD WE'LL GO SLEDDING OFF THE ROOF.
OUT OF THE WAY! HERE COME THE SWEDES!

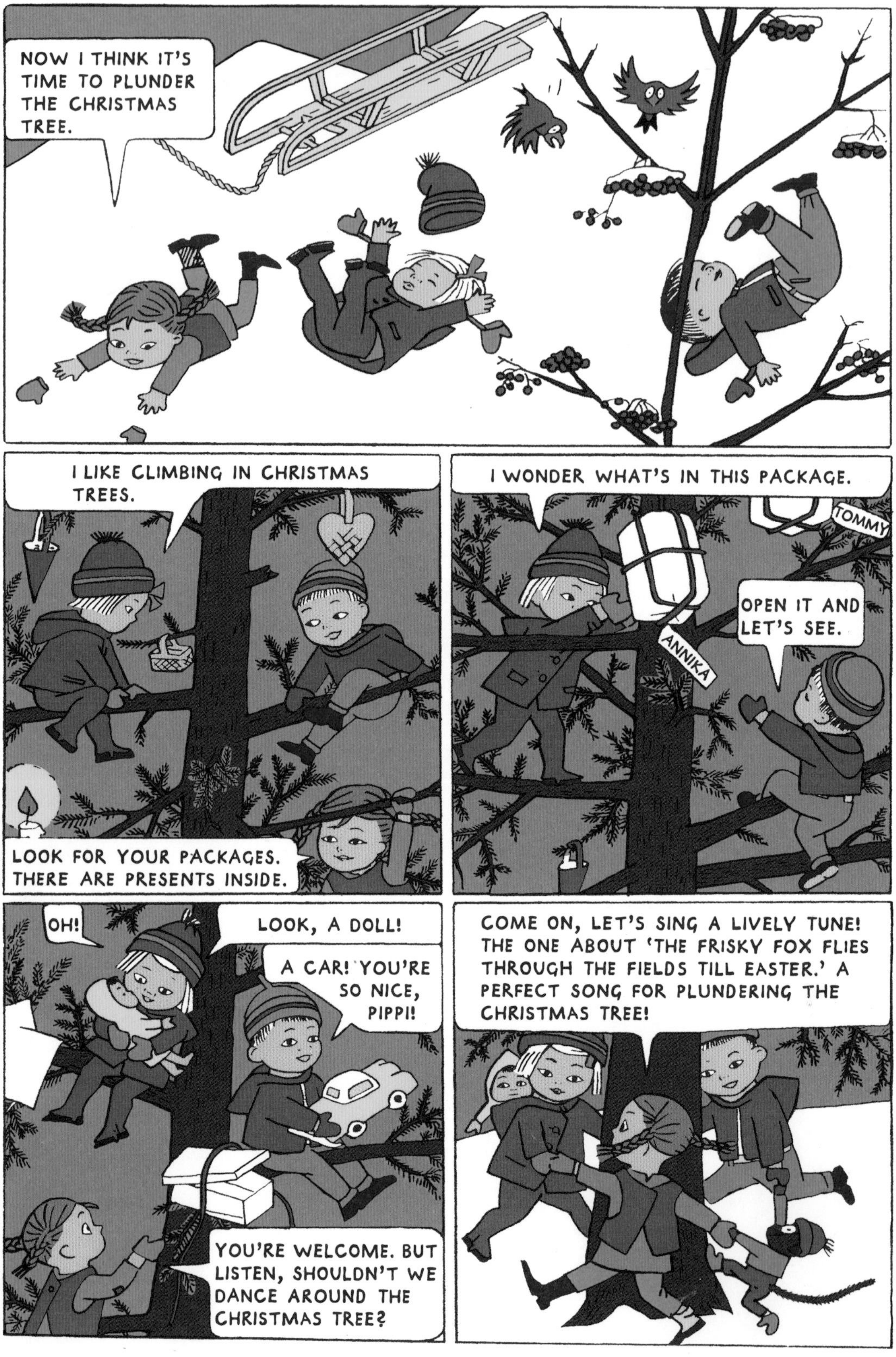
NOW I THINK IT'S TIME TO PLUNDER THE CHRISTMAS TREE.
I LIKE CLIMBING IN CHRISTMAS TREES.
LOOK FOR YOUR PACKAGES. THERE ARE PRESENTS INSIDE.
I WONDER WHAT'S IN THIS PACKAGE.
TOMMY
ANNIKA
OPEN IT AND LET'S SEE.
OH!
LOOK, A DOLL!
A CAR! YOU'RE SO NICE, PIPPI!
YOU'RE WELCOME. BUT LISTEN, SHOULDN'T WE DANCE AROUND THE CHRISTMAS TREE?
COME ON, LET'S SING A LIVELY TUNE! THE ONE ABOUT 'THE FRISKY FOX FLIES THROUGH THE FIELDS TILL EASTER.' A PERFECT SONG FOR PLUNDERING THE CHRISTMAS TREE!

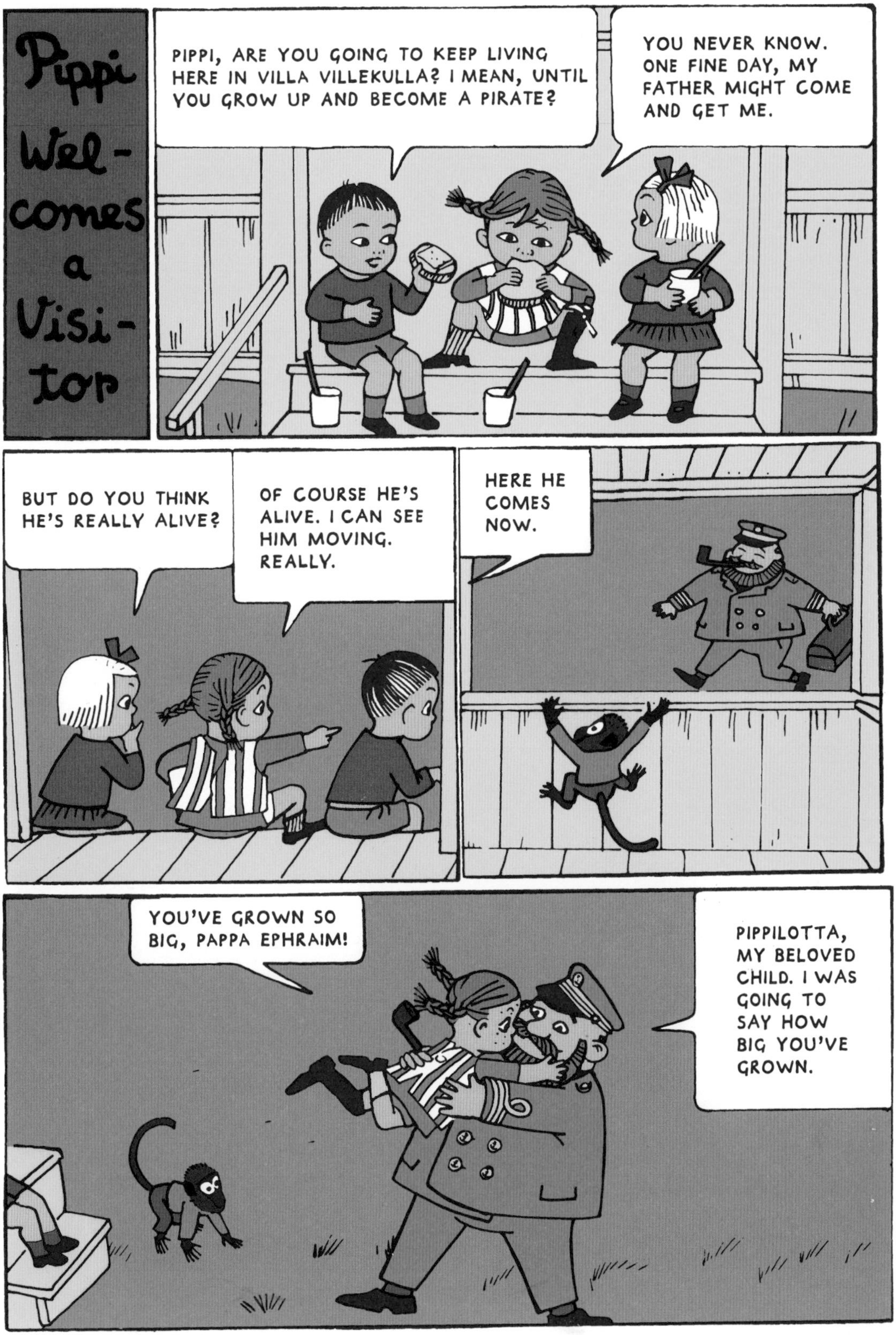
Pippi Welcomes a Visitor
PIPPI, ARE YOU GOING TO KEEP LIVING HERE IN VILLA VILLEKULLA? I MEAN, UNTIL YOU GROW UP AND BECOME A PIRATE?
YOU NEVER KNOW. ONE FINE DAY, MY FATHER MIGHT COME AND GET ME.
BUT DO YOU THINK HE'S REALLY ALIVE?
OF COURSE HE'S ALIVE. I CAN SEE HIM MOVING. REALLY.
HERE HE COMES NOW.
YOU'VE GROWN SO BIG, PAPPA EPHRAIM!
PIPPILOTTA, MY BELOVED CHILD. I WAS GOING TO SAY HOW BIG YOU'VE GROWN.

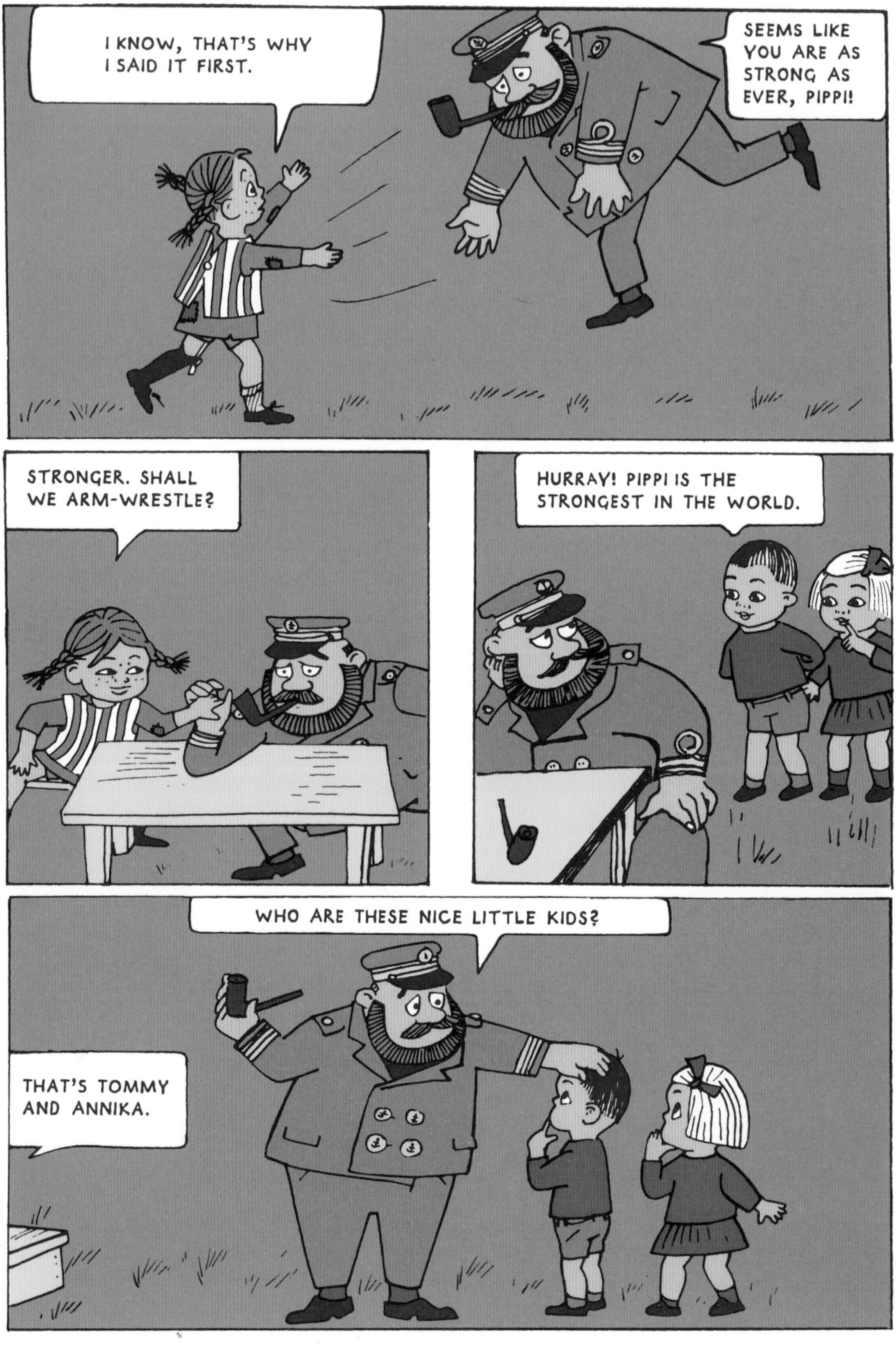
I KNOW, THAT'S WHY I SAID IT FIRST.
SEEMS LIKE YOU ARE AS STRONG AS EVER, PIPPI!
STRONGER. SHALL WE ARM-WRESTLE?
HURRAY! PIPPI IS THE STRONGEST IN THE WORLD.
WHO ARE THESE NICE LITTLE KIDS?
THAT'S TOMMY AND ANNIKA.

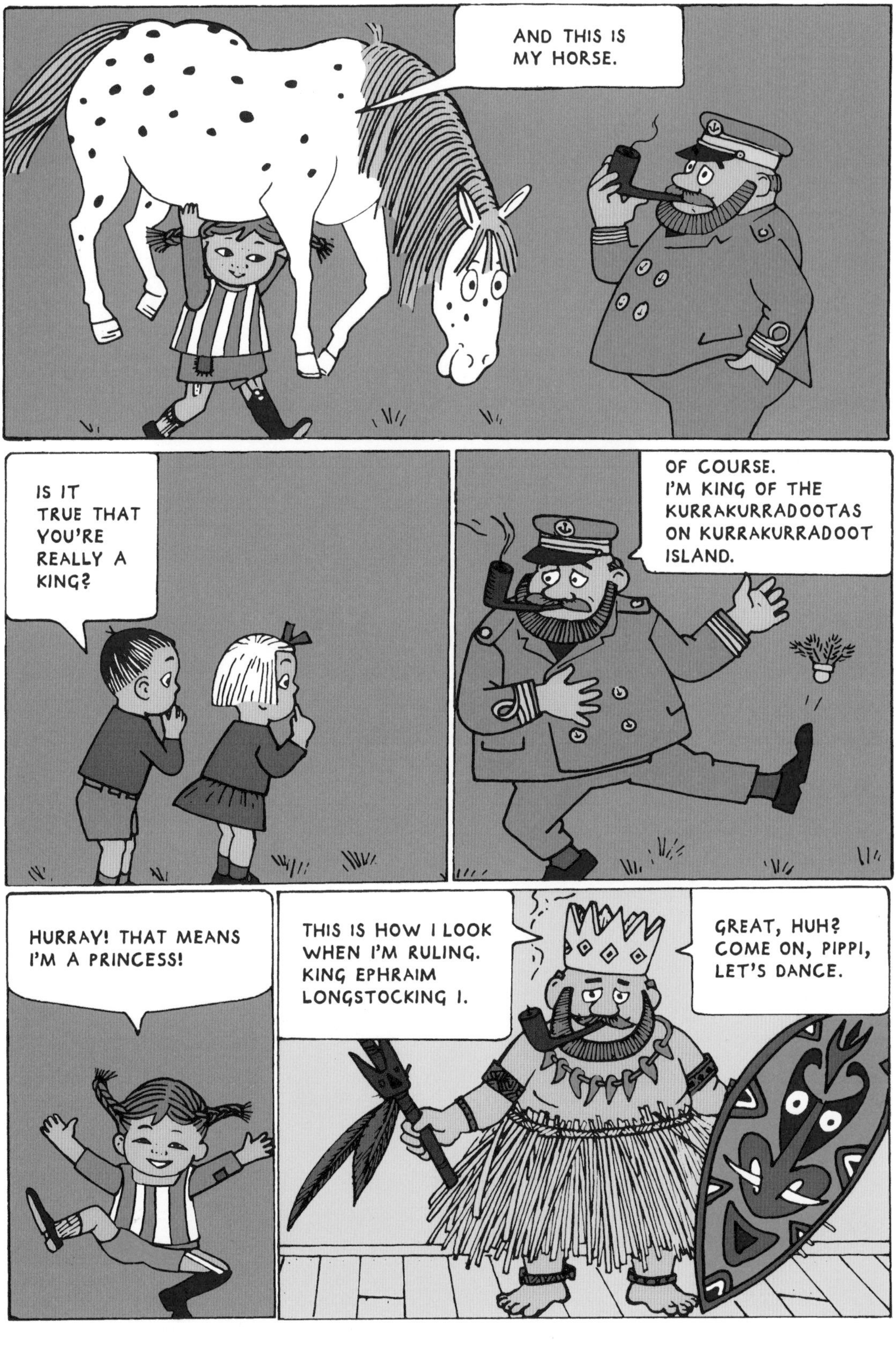
AND THIS IS MY HORSE.
IS IT TRUE THAT YOU'RE REALLY A KING?
OF COURSE. I'M KING OF THE KURRAKURRADOOTAS ON KURRAKURRADOOT ISLAND.
HURRAY! THAT MEANS I'M A PRINCESS!
THIS IS HOW I LOOK WHEN I'M RULING. KING EPHRAIM LONGSTOCKING I.
GREAT, HUH? COME ON, PIPPI, LET'S DANCE.

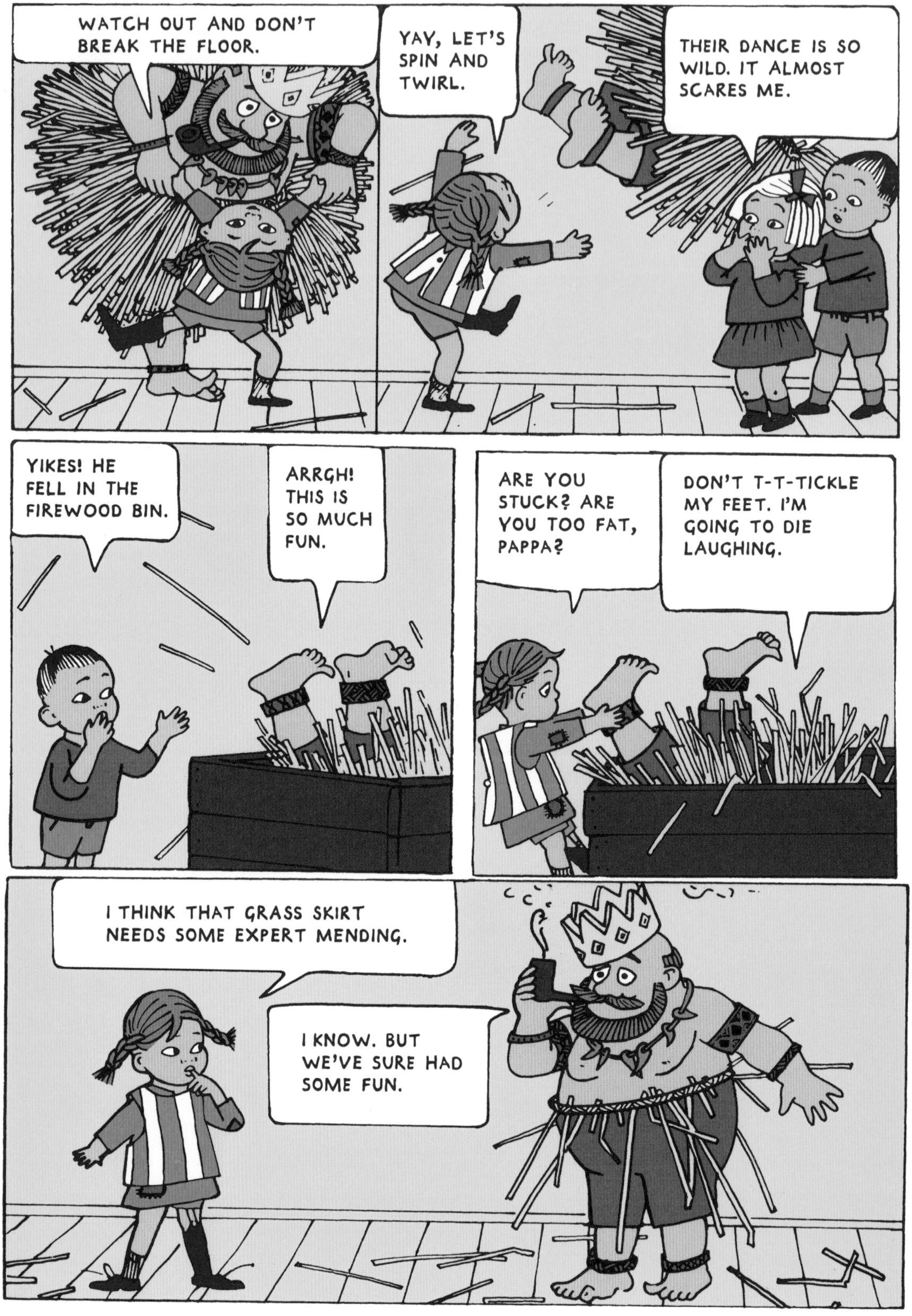

WATCH OUT AND DON'T BREAK THE FLOOR.
YAY, LET'S SPIN AND TWIRL.
THEIR DANCE IS SO WILD. IT ALMOST SCARES ME.
YIKES! HE FELL IN THE FIREWOOD BIN.
ARRGH! THIS IS SO MUCH FUN.
ARE YOU STUCK? ARE YOU TOO FAT, PAPPA?
DON'T T-T-TICKLE MY FEET. I'M GOING TO DIE LAUGHING.
I THINK THAT GRASS SKIRT NEEDS SOME EXPERT MENDING.
I KNOW. BUT WE'VE SURE HAD SOME FUN.

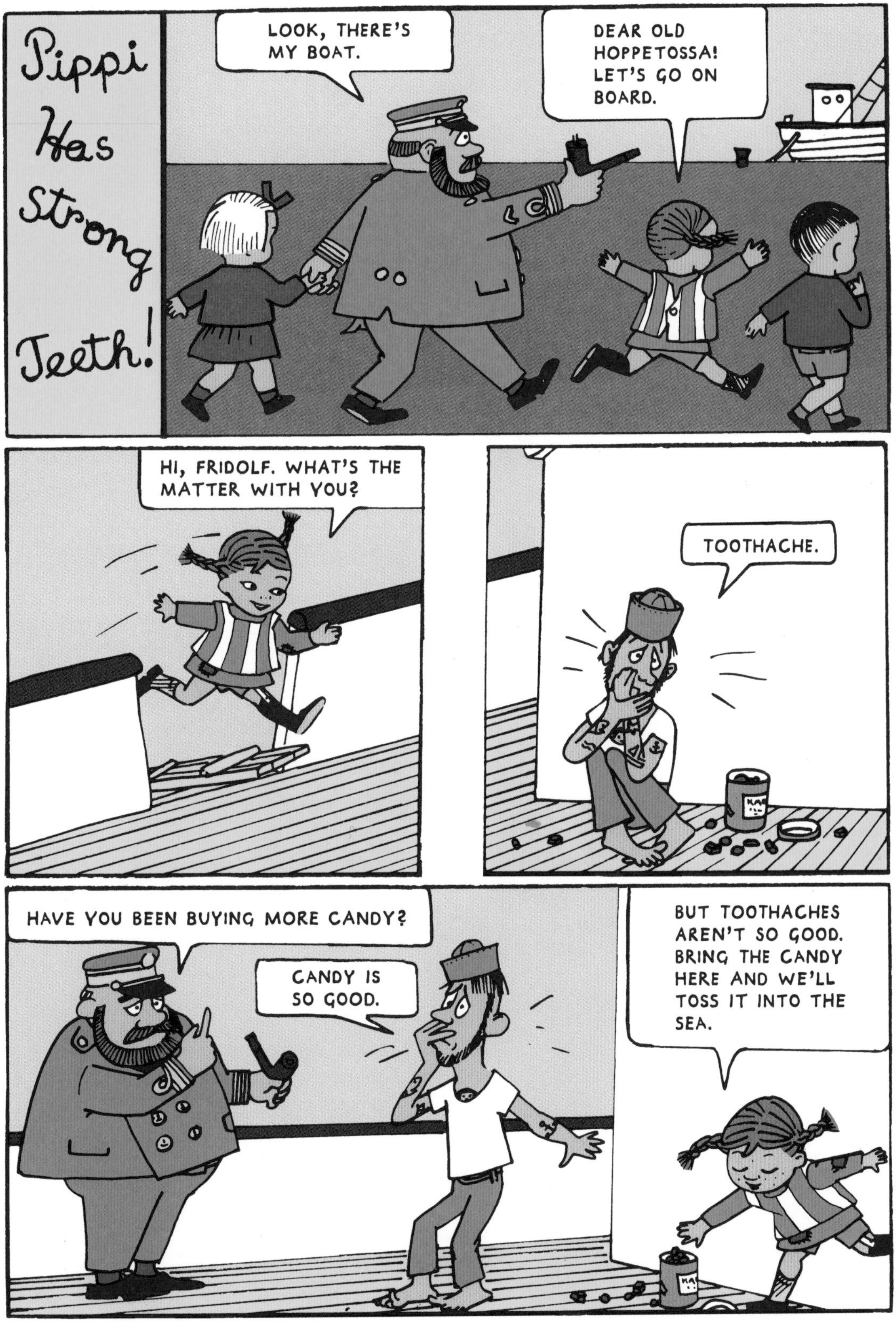
Pippi Has Strong Teeth!
LOOK, THERE'S MY BOAT.
DEAR OLD HOPPETOSSA! LET'S GO ON BOARD.
HI, FRIDOLF. WHAT'S THE MATTER WITH YOU?
TOOTHACHE.
HAVE YOU BEEN BUYING MORE CANDY?
CANDY IS SO GOOD.
BUT TOOTHACHES AREN'T SO GOOD. BRING THE CANDY HERE AND WE'LL TOSS IT INTO THE SEA.

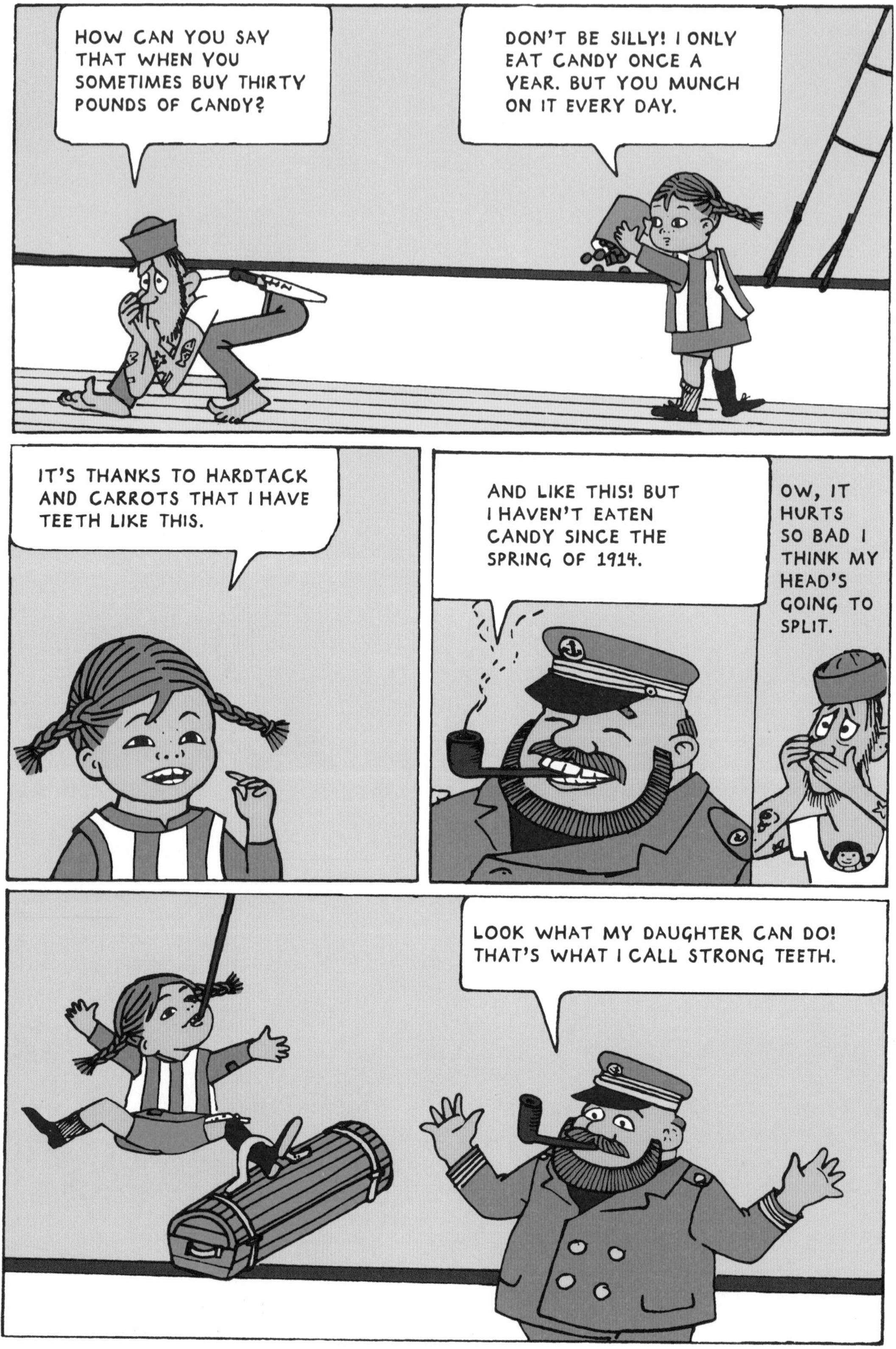
HOW CAN YOU SAY THAT WHEN YOU SOMETIMES BUY THIRTY POUNDS OF CANDY?
DON'T BE SILLY! I ONLY EAT CANDY ONCE A YEAR. BUT YOU MUNCH ON IT EVERY DAY.
IT'S THANKS TO HARDTACK AND CARROTS THAT I HAVE TEETH LIKE THIS.
AND LIKE THIS! BUT I HAVEN'T EATEN CANDY SINCE THE SPRING OF 1914.
OW, IT HURTS SO BAD I THINK MY HEAD'S GOING TO SPLIT.
LOOK WHAT MY DAUGHTER CAN DO! THAT'S WHAT I CALL STRONG TEETH.

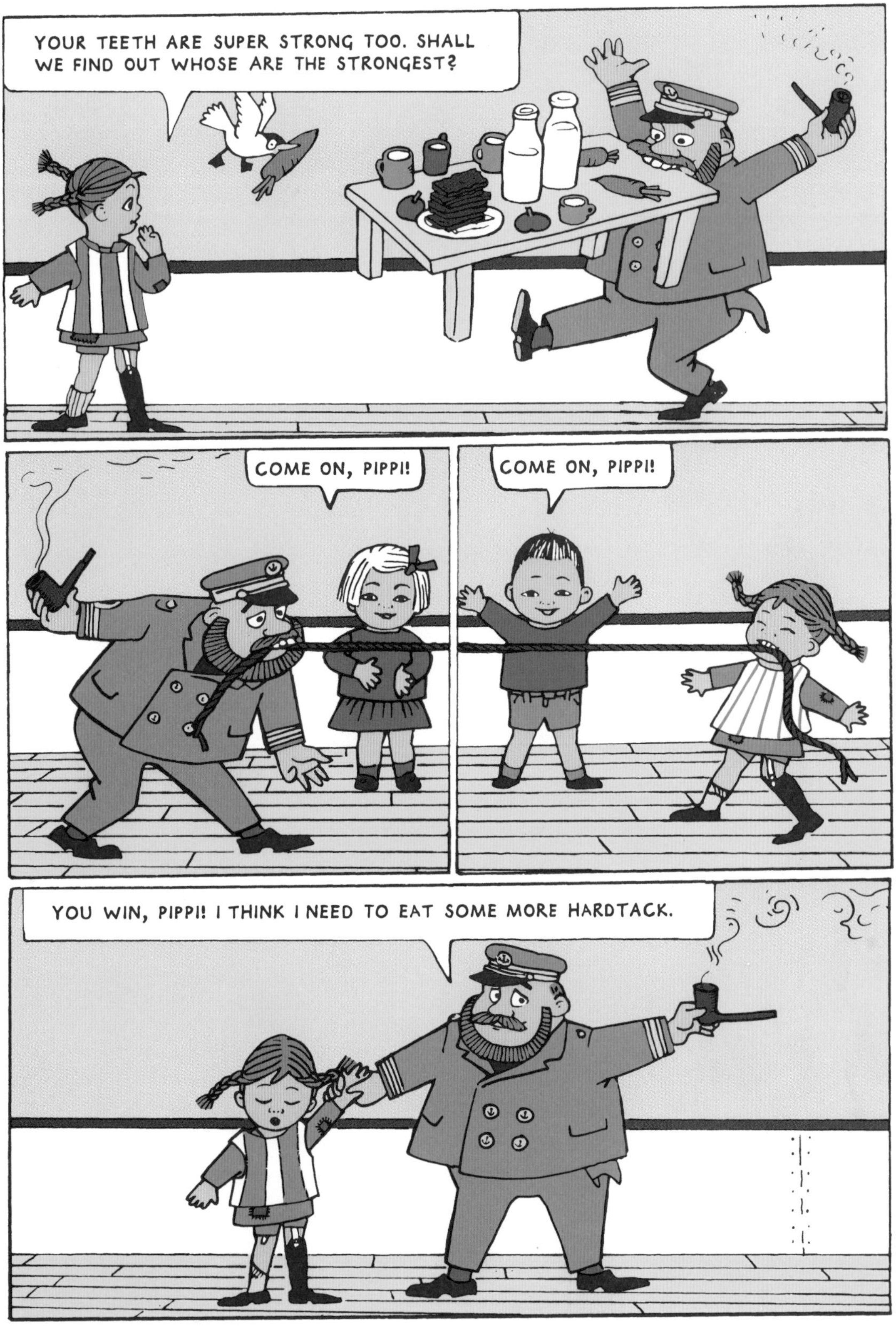
YOUR TEETH ARE SUPER STRONG TOO. SHALL WE FIND OUT WHOSE ARE THE STRONGEST?
COME ON, PIPPI!
COME ON, PIPPI!
YOU WIN, PIPPI! I THINK I NEED TO EAT SOME MORE HARDTACK.

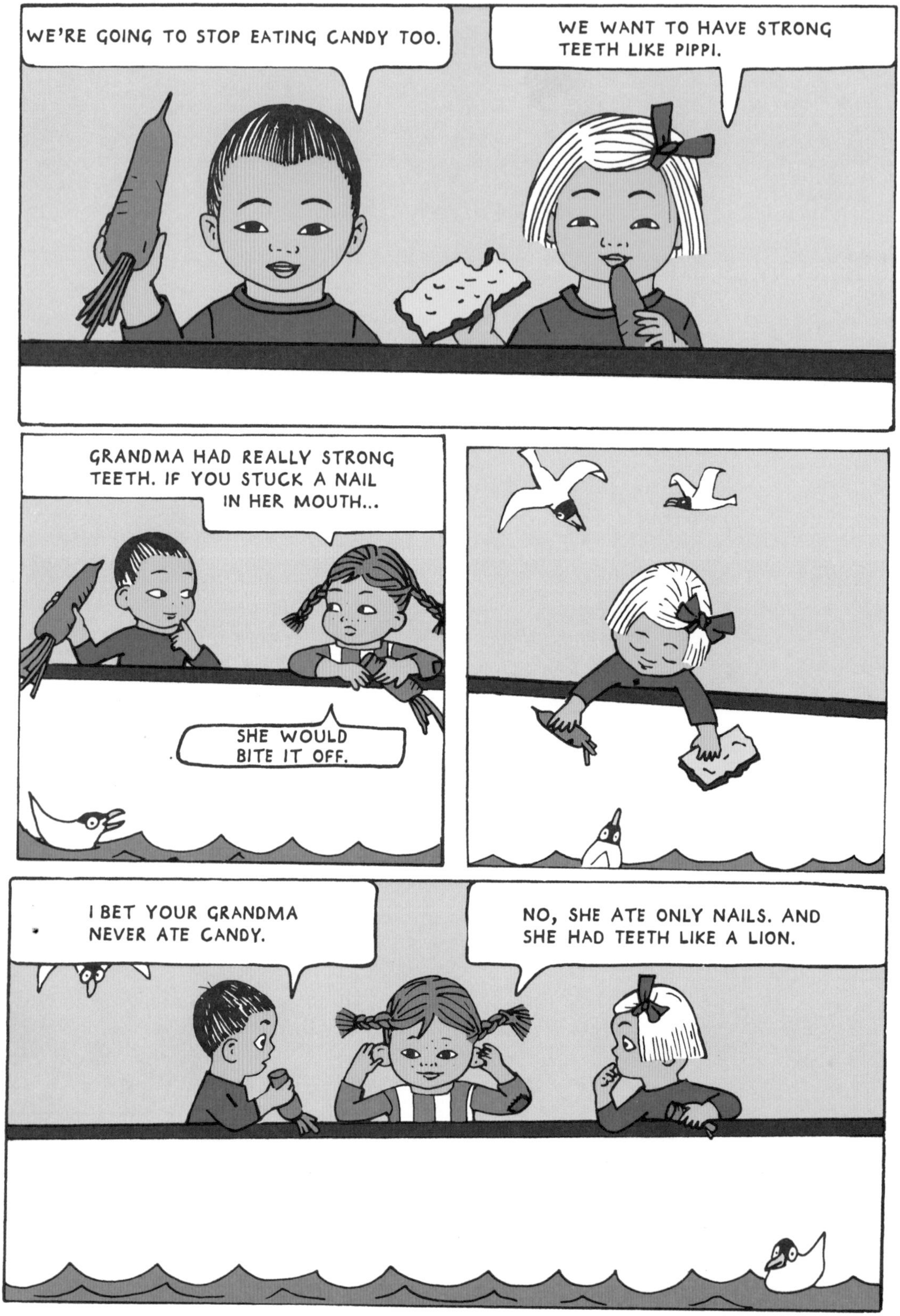
WE'RE GOING TO STOP EATING CANDY TOO.
WE WANT TO HAVE STRONG TEETH LIKE PIPPI.
GRANDMA HAD REALLY STRONG TEETH. IF YOU STUCK A NAIL IN HER MOUTH...
SHE WOULD BITE IT OFF.
I BET YOUR GRANDMA NEVER ATE CANDY.
NO, SHE ATE ONLY NAILS. AND SHE HAD TEETH LIKE A LION.

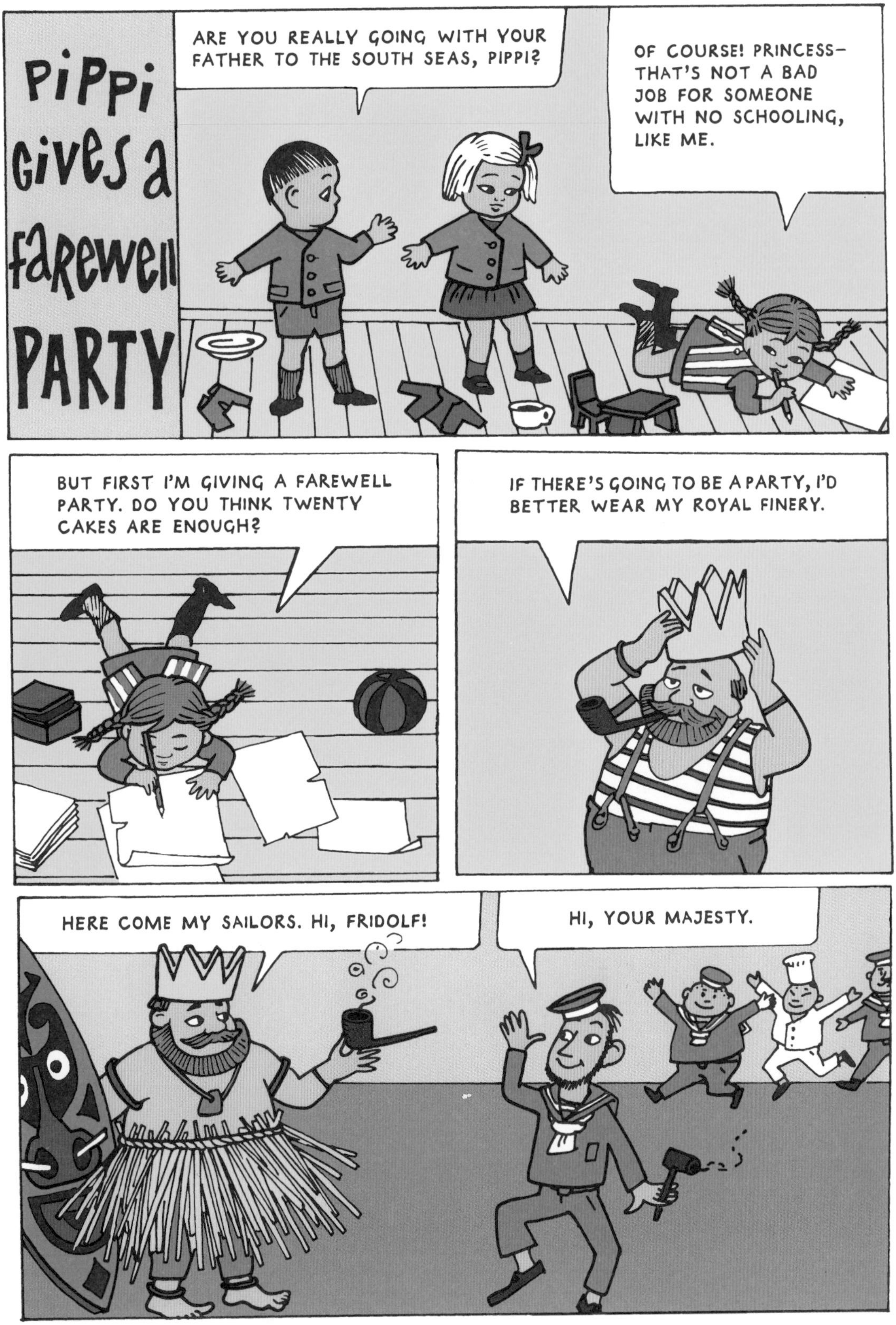
PIPPI GIVES A FAREWELL PARTY
ARE YOU REALLY GOING WITH YOUR FATHER TO THE SOUTH SEAS, PIPPI?
OF COURSE! PRINCESS—THAT'S NOT A BAD JOB FOR SOMEONE WITH NO SCHOOLING, LIKE ME.
BUT FIRST I'M GIVING A FAREWELL PARTY. DO YOU THINK TWENTY CAKES ARE ENOUGH?
IF THERE'S GOING TO BE A PARTY, I'D BETTER WEAR MY ROYAL FINERY.
HERE COME MY SAILORS. HI, FRIDOLF!
HI, YOUR MAJESTY.

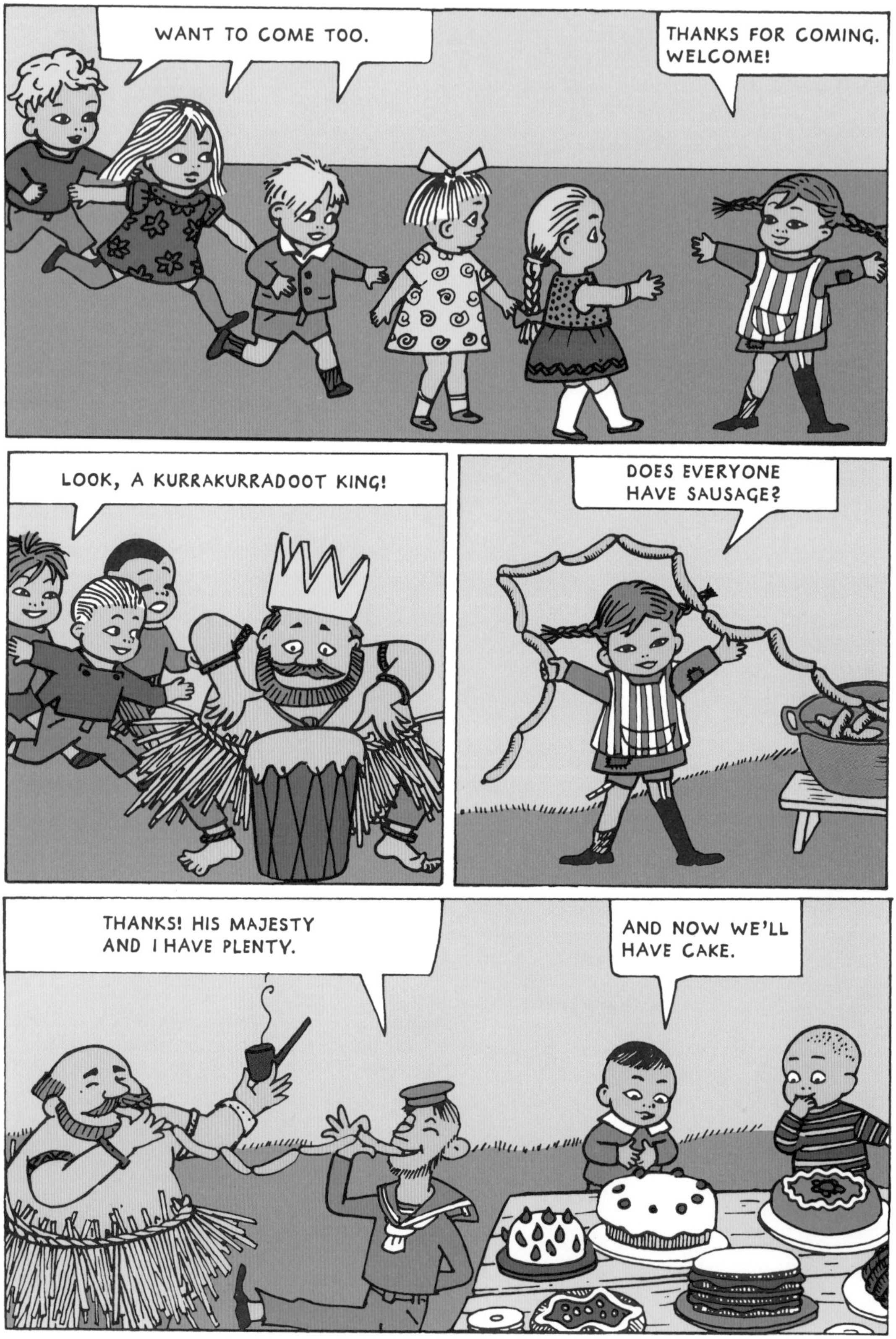
WANT TO COME TOO.
THANKS FOR COMING. WELCOME!
LOOK, A KURRAKURRADOOT KING!
DOES EVERYONE HAVE SAUSAGE?
THANKS! HIS MAJESTY AND I HAVE PLENTY.
AND NOW WE'LL HAVE CAKE.

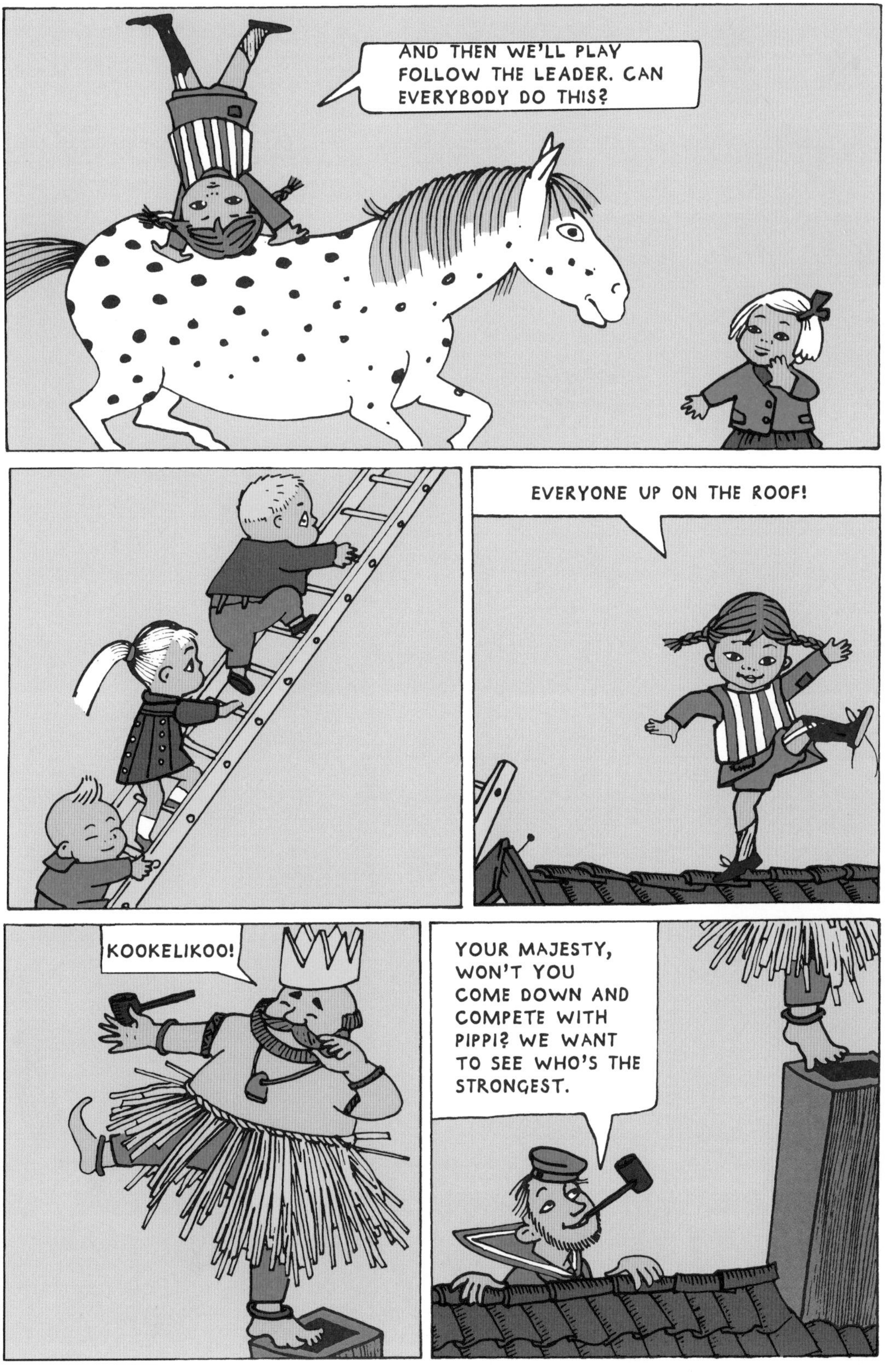
AND THEN WE'LL PLAY FOLLOW THE LEADER. CAN EVERYBODY DO THIS?
EVERYONE UP ON THE ROOF!
KOOKELIKOO!
YOUR MAJESTY, WON'T YOU COME DOWN AND COMPETE WITH PIPPI? WE WANT TO SEE WHO'S THE STRONGEST.

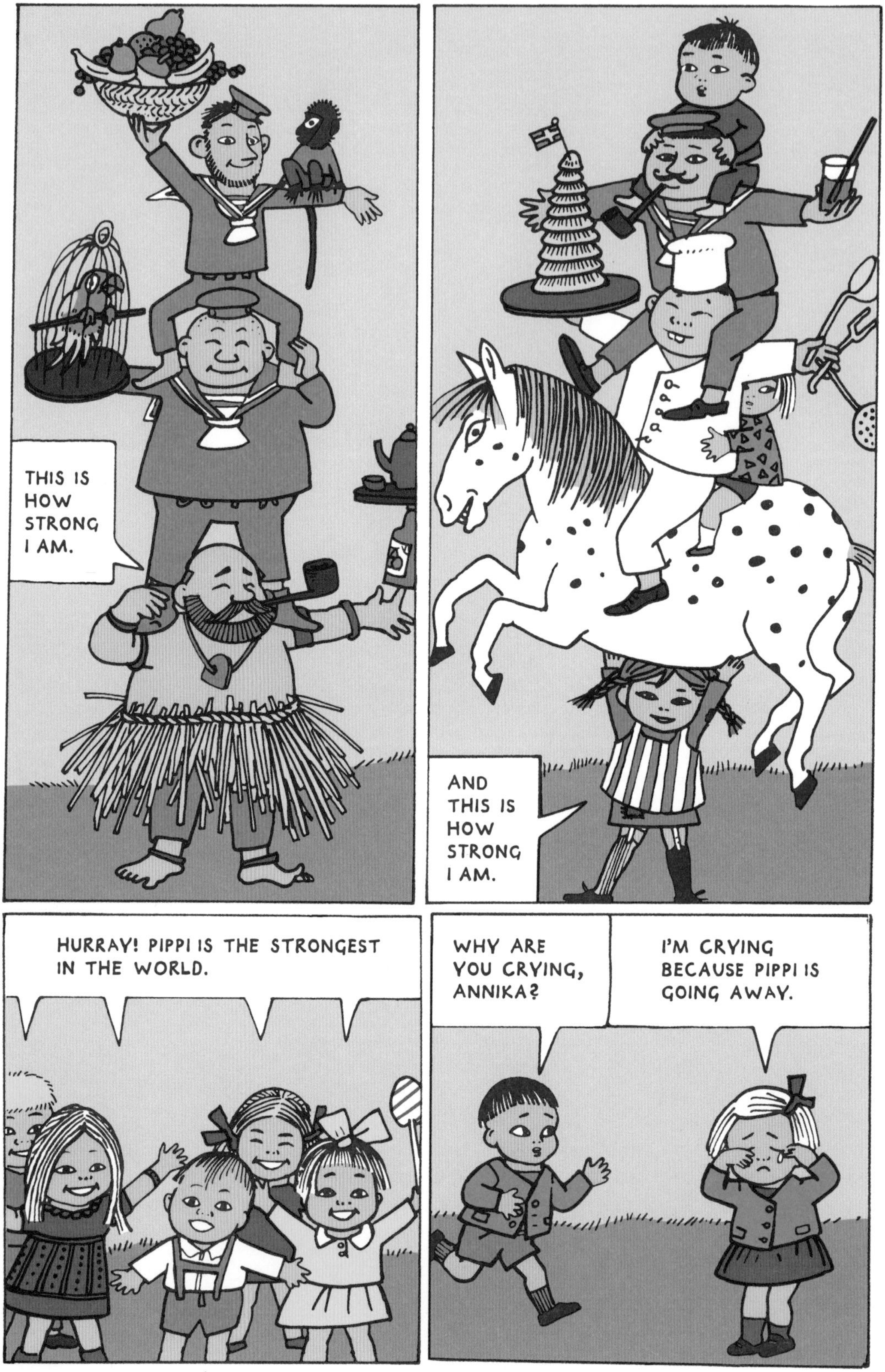
THIS IS HOW STRONG I AM.
AND THIS IS HOW STRONG I AM.
HURRAY! PIPPI IS THE STRONGEST IN THE WORLD.
WHY ARE YOU CRYING, ANNIKA?
I'M CRYING BECAUSE PIPPI IS GOING AWAY.

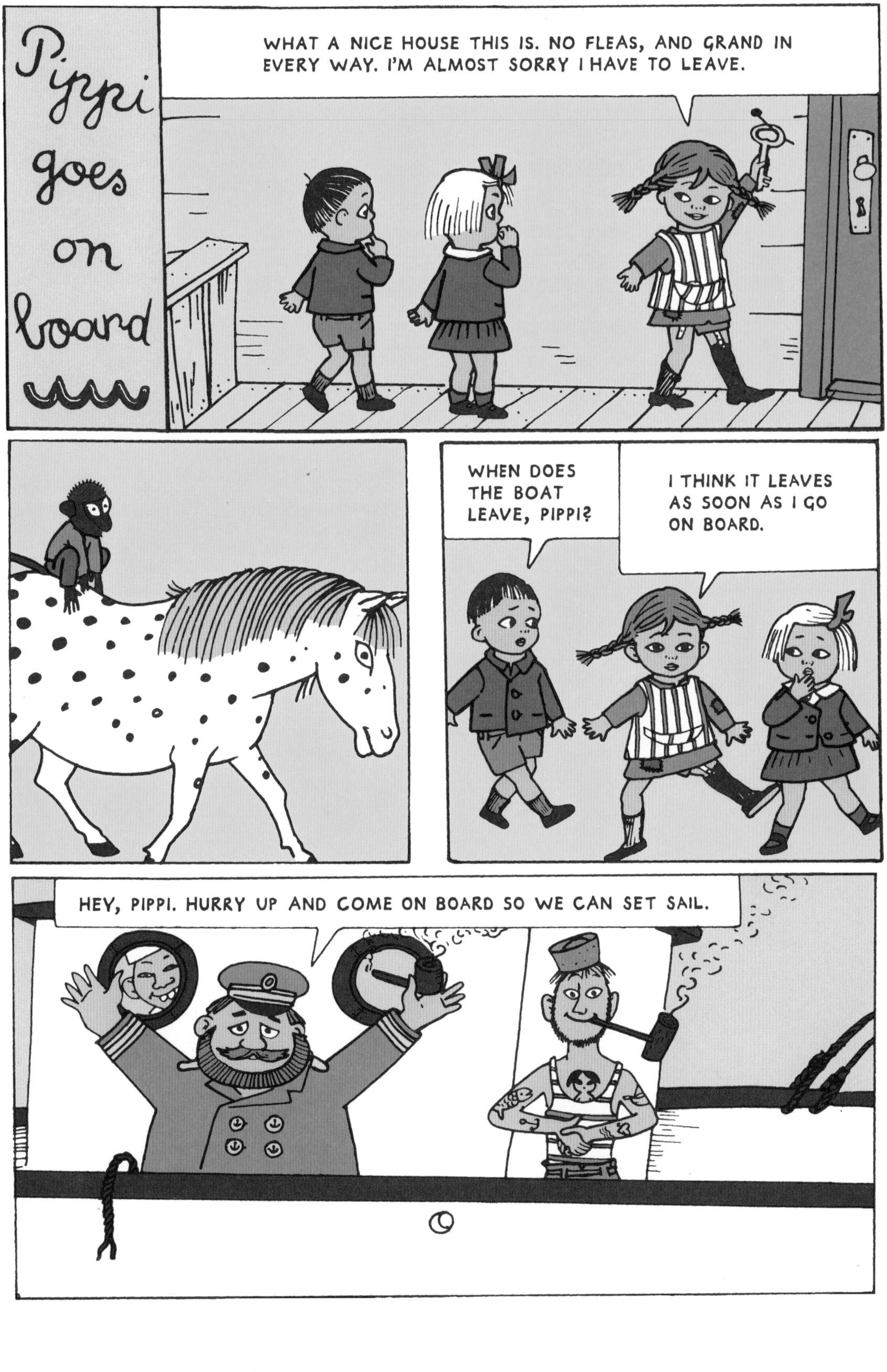
Pippi goes on board
WHAT A NICE HOUSE THIS IS. NO FLEAS, AND GRAND IN EVERY WAY. I'M ALMOST SORRY I HAVE TO LEAVE.
WHEN DOES THE BOAT LEAVE, PIPPI?
I THINK IT LEAVES AS SOON AS I GO ON BOARD.
HEY, PIPPI. HURRY UP AND COME ON BOARD SO WE CAN SET SAIL.

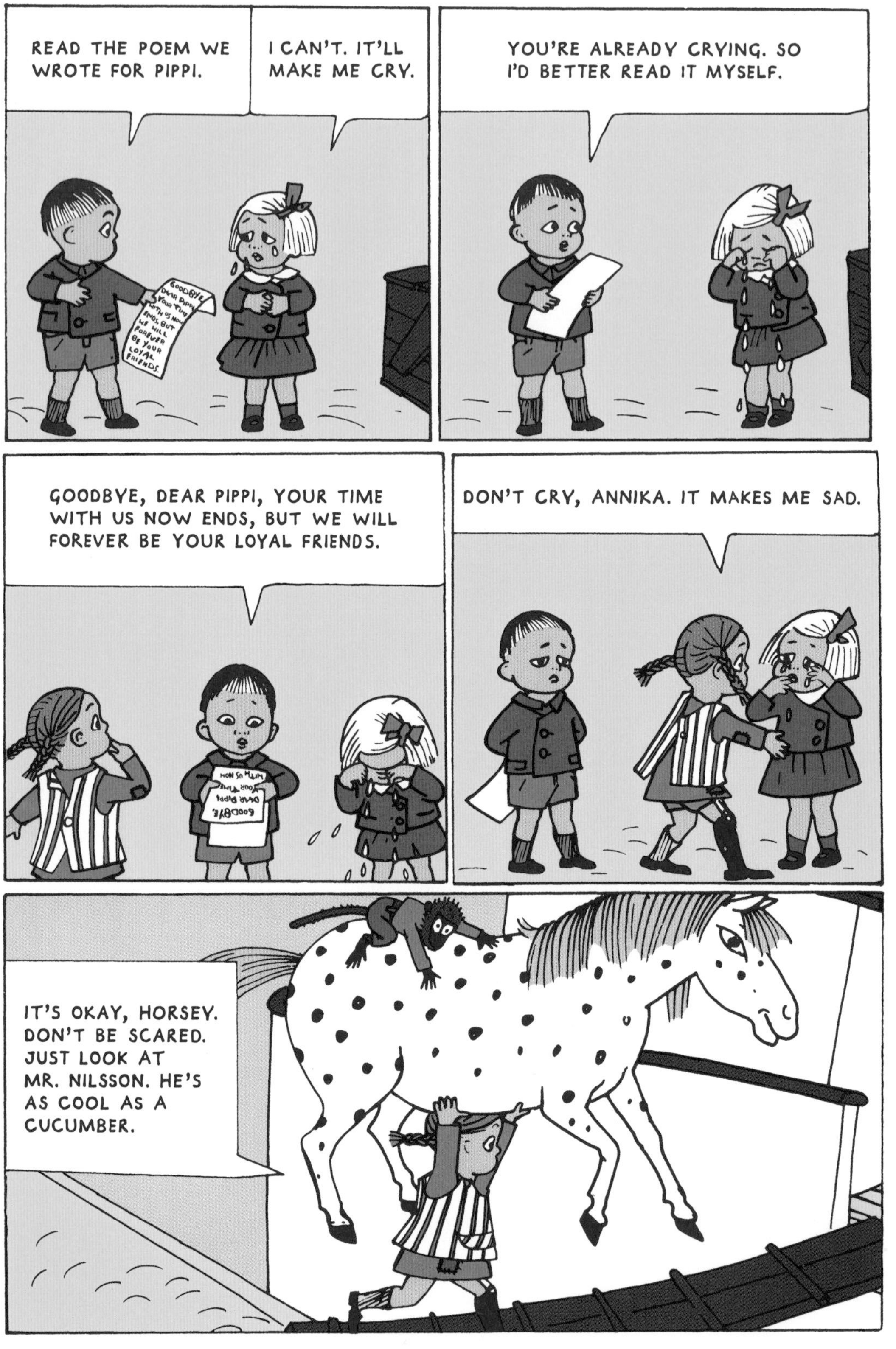
READ THE POEM WE WROTE FOR PIPPI.
I CAN'T. IT'LL MAKE ME CRY.
GOODBYE DEAR PIPPI YOUR TIME WITH US NOW ENDS, BUT WE WILL FOREVER BE YOUR LOYAL FRIENDS.
YOU'RE ALREADY CRYING. SO I'D BETTER READ IT MYSELF.
GOODBYE, DEAR PIPPI, YOUR TIME WITH US NOW ENDS, BUT WE WILL FOREVER BE YOUR LOYAL FRIENDS.
DON'T CRY, ANNIKA. IT MAKES ME SAD.
IT'S OKAY, HORSEY. DON'T BE SCARED. JUST LOOK AT MR. NILSSON. HE'S AS COOL AS A CUCUMBER.

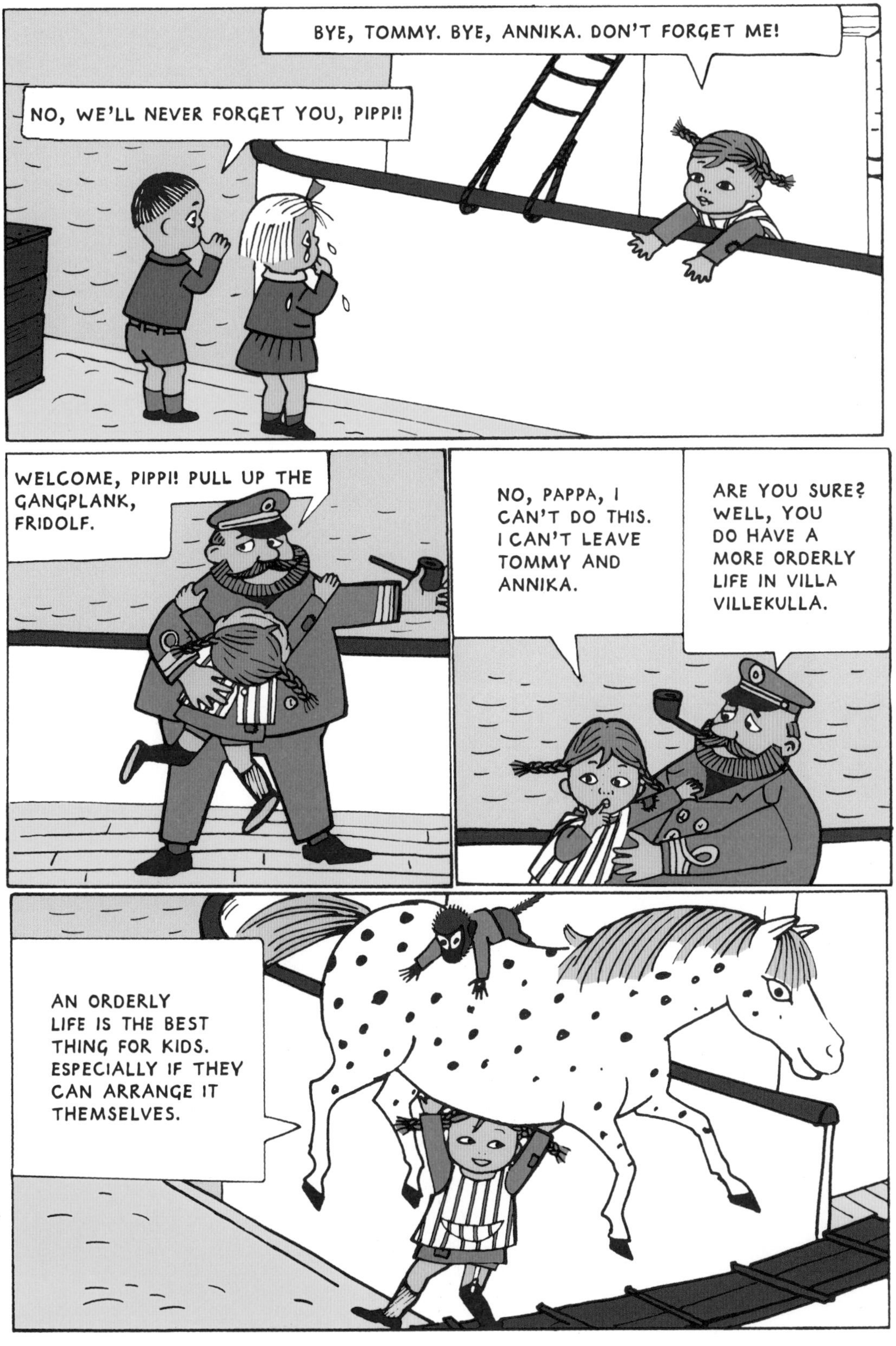
BYE, TOMMY. BYE, ANNIKA. DON'T FORGET ME!
NO, WE'LL NEVER FORGET YOU, PIPPI!
WELCOME, PIPPI! PULL UP THE GANGPLANK, FRIDOLF.
NO, PAPPA, I CAN'T DO THIS. I CAN'T LEAVE TOMMY AND ANNIKA.
ARE YOU SURE? WELL, YOU DO HAVE A MORE ORDERLY LIFE IN VILLA VILLEKULLA.
AN ORDERLY LIFE IS THE BEST THING FOR KIDS. ESPECIALLY IF THEY CAN ARRANGE IT THEMSELVES.

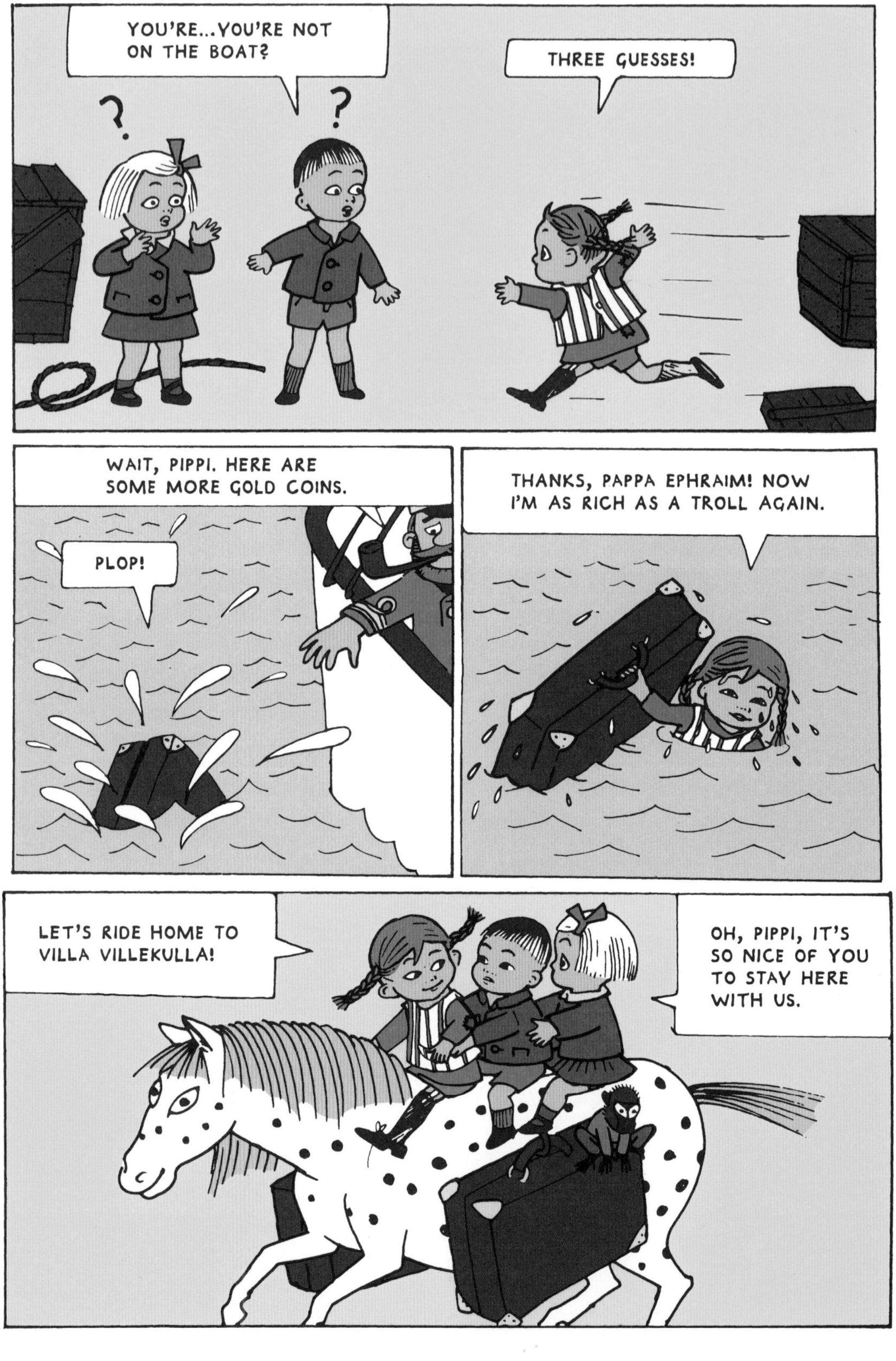
YOU'RE...YOU'RE NOT ON THE BOAT?
THREE GUESSES!
WAIT, PIPPI. HERE ARE SOME MORE GOLD COINS.
PLOP!
THANKS, PAPPA EPHRAIM! NOW I'M AS RICH AS A TROLL AGAIN.
LET'S RIDE HOME TO VILLA VILLEKULLA!
OH, PIPPI, IT'S SO NICE OF YOU TO STAY HERE WITH US.

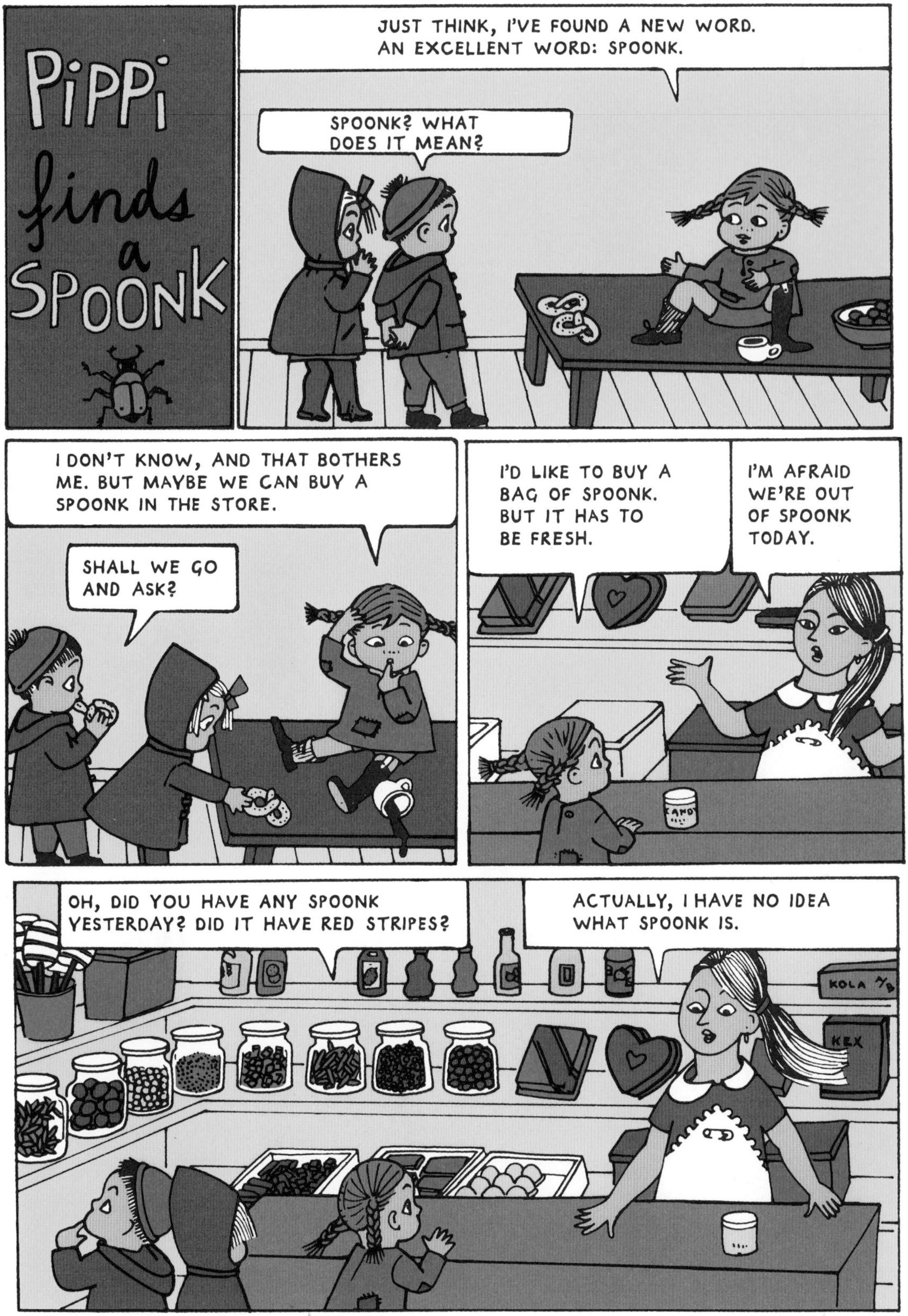
Pippi finds a Spoonk
JUST THINK, I'VE FOUND A NEW WORD. AN EXCELLENT WORD: SPOONK.
SPOONK? WHAT DOES IT MEAN?
I DON'T KNOW, AND THAT BOTHERS ME. BUT MAYBE WE CAN BUY A SPOONK IN THE STORE.
SHALL WE GO AND ASK?
I'D LIKE TO BUY A BAG OF SPOONK. BUT IT HAS TO BE FRESH.
I'M AFRAID WE'RE OUT OF SPOONK TODAY.
OH, DID YOU HAVE ANY SPOONK YESTERDAY? DID IT HAVE RED STRIPES?
ACTUALLY, I HAVE NO IDEA WHAT SPOONK IS.
KOLA
KEX
CANDY

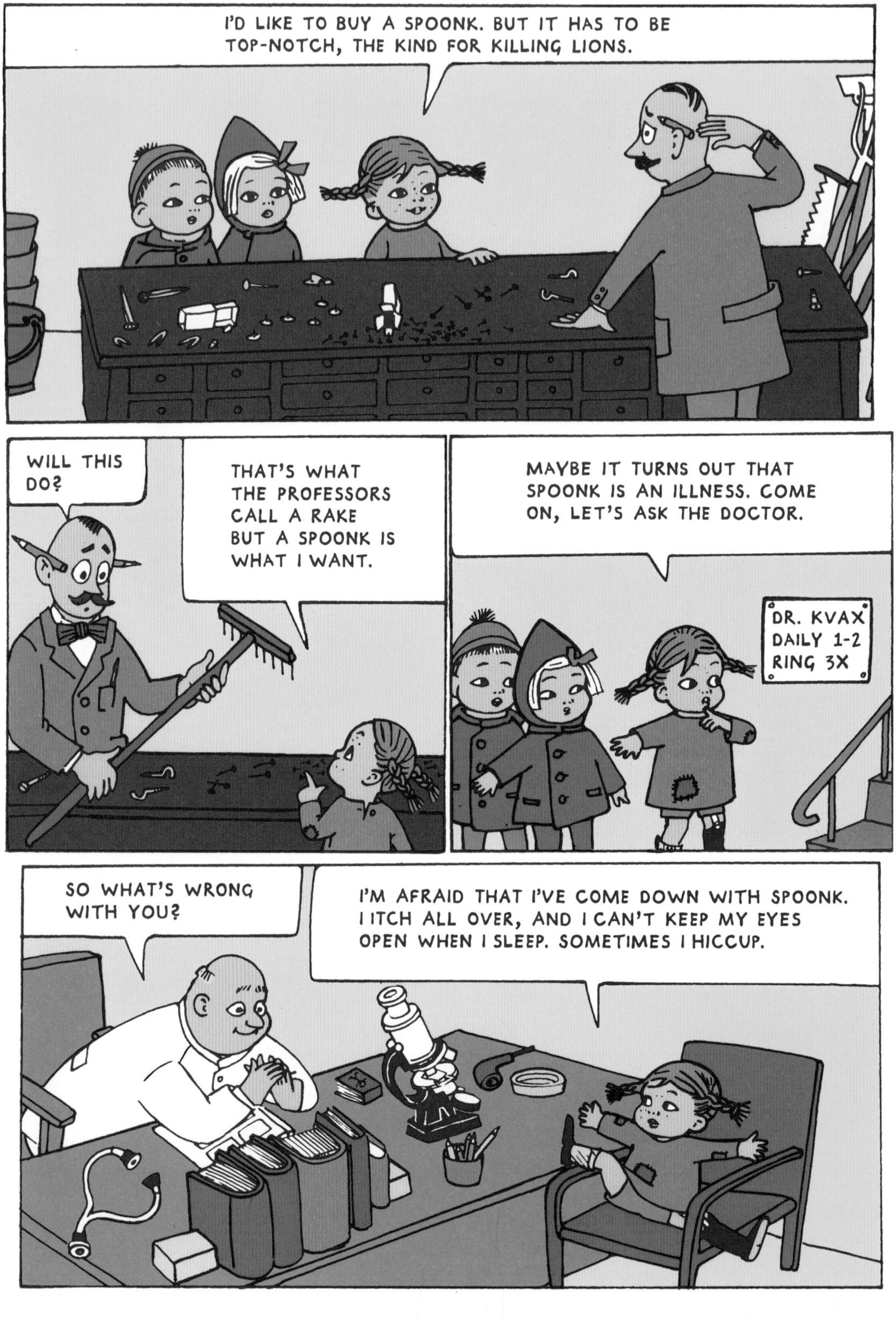
I'D LIKE TO BUY A SPOONK. BUT IT HAS TO BE TOP-NOTCH, THE KIND FOR KILLING LIONS.
WILL THIS DO?
THAT'S WHAT THE PROFESSORS CALL A RAKE BUT A SPOONK IS WHAT I WANT.
MAYBE IT TURNS OUT THAT SPOONK IS AN ILLNESS. COME ON, LET'S ASK THE DOCTOR.
DR. KVAX DAILY 1-2 RING 3X
SO WHAT'S WRONG WITH YOU?
I'M AFRAID THAT I'VE COME DOWN WITH SPOONK. I ITCH ALL OVER, AND I CAN'T KEEP MY EYES OPEN WHEN I SLEEP. SOMETIMES I HICCUP.

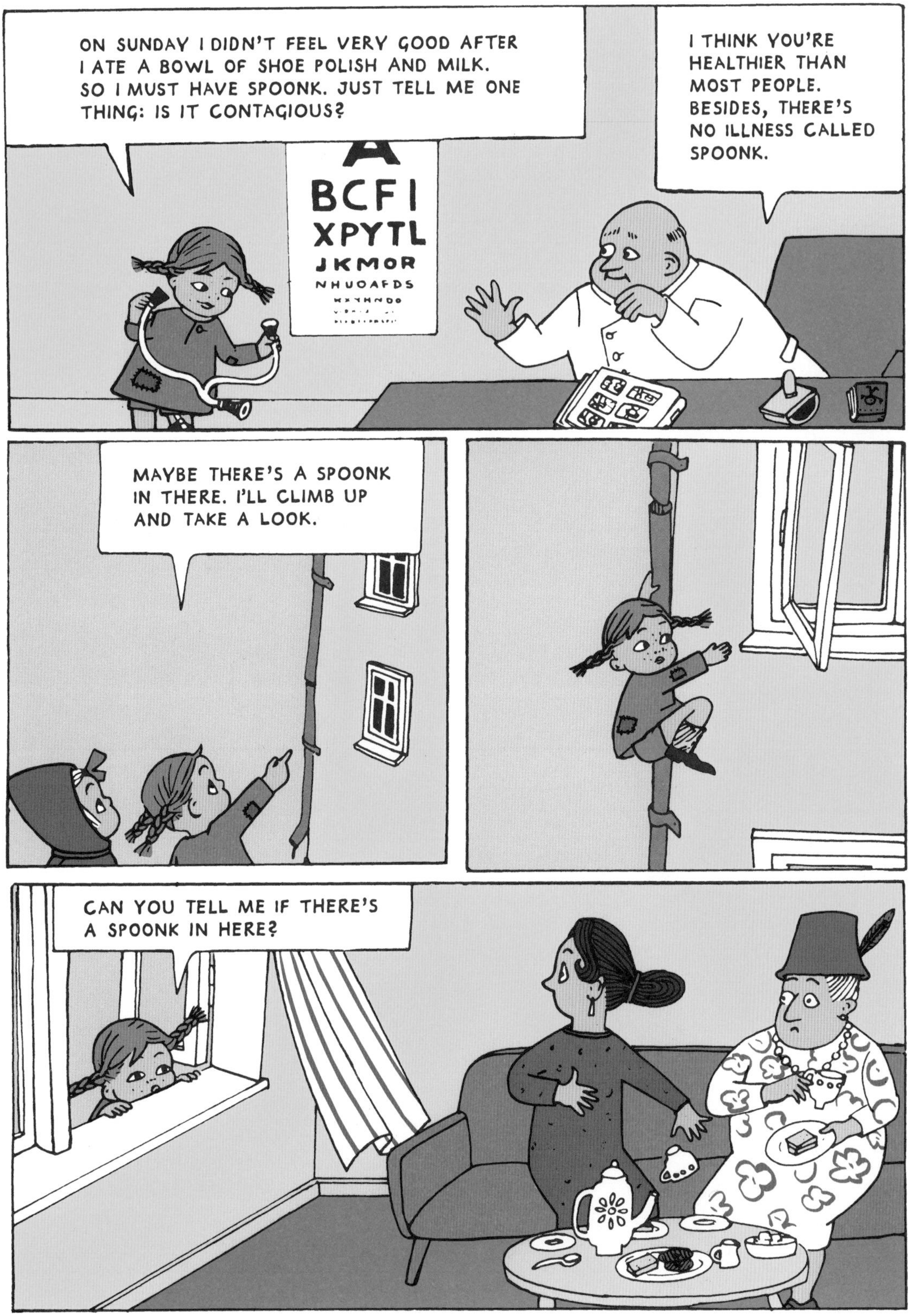
ON SUNDAY I DIDN'T FEEL VERY GOOD AFTER I ATE A BOWL OF SHOE POLISH AND MILK. SO I MUST HAVE SPOONK. JUST TELL ME ONE THING: IS IT CONTAGIOUS?
A
BCFI
XPYTL
JKMOR
NHUOAFDS
I THINK YOU'RE HEALTHIER THAN MOST PEOPLE. BESIDES, THERE'S NO ILLNESS CALLED SPOONK.
MAYBE THERE'S A SPOONK IN THERE. I'LL CLIMB UP AND TAKE A LOOK.
CAN YOU TELL ME IF THERE'S A SPOONK IN HERE?

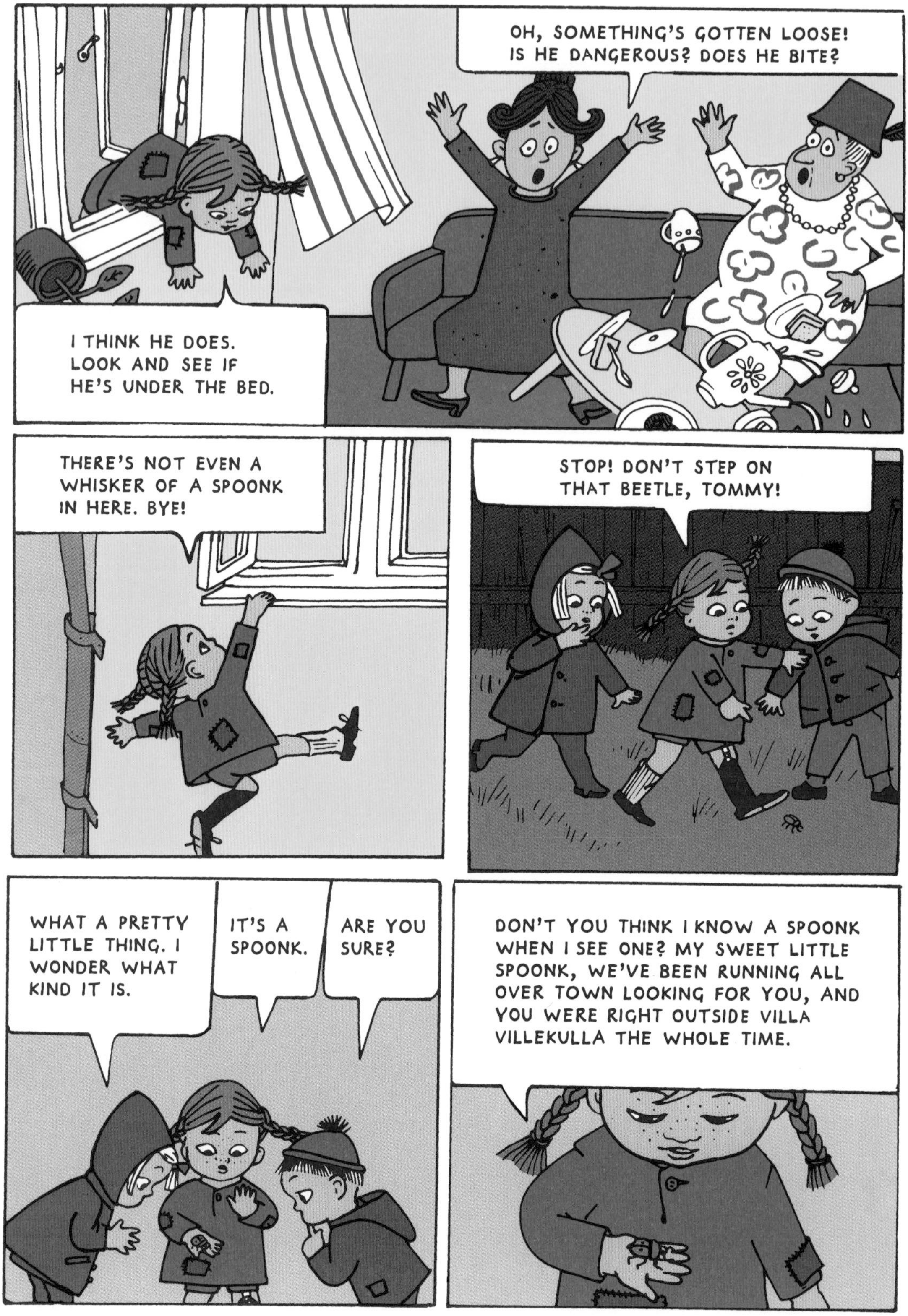
OH, SOMETHING'S GOTTEN LOOSE! IS HE DANGEROUS? DOES HE BITE?
I THINK HE DOES. LOOK AND SEE IF HE'S UNDER THE BED.
THERE'S NOT EVEN A WHISKER OF A SPOONK IN HERE. BYE!
STOP! DON'T STEP ON THAT BEETLE, TOMMY!
WHAT A PRETTY LITTLE THING. I WONDER WHAT KIND IT IS.
IT'S A SPOONK.
ARE YOU SURE?
DON'T YOU THINK I KNOW A SPOONK WHEN I SEE ONE? MY SWEET LITTLE SPOONK, WE'VE BEEN RUNNING ALL OVER TOWN LOOKING FOR YOU, AND YOU WERE RIGHT OUTSIDE VILLA VILLEKULLA THE WHOLE TIME.

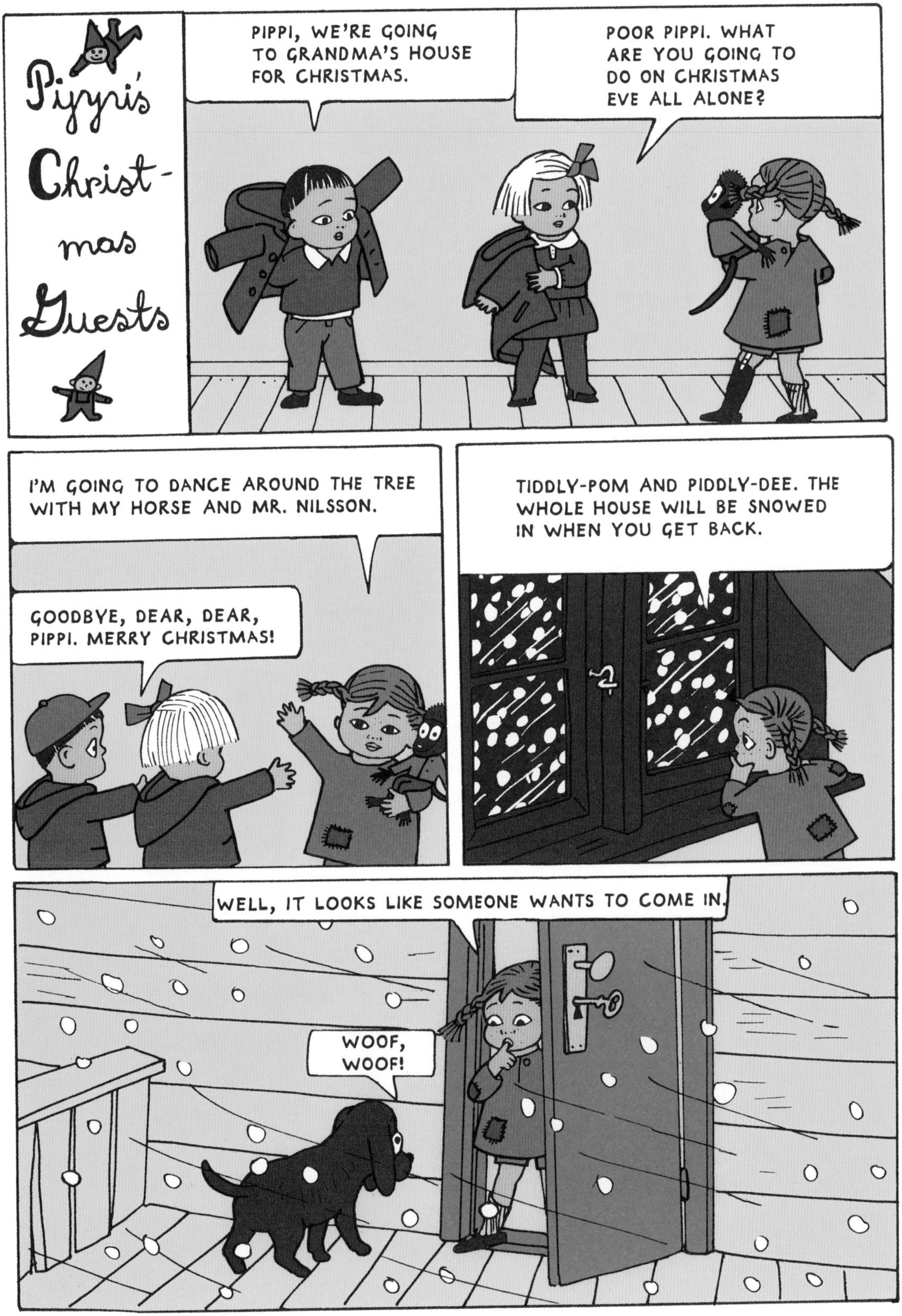
Pippi's Christmas Guests
PIPPI, WE'RE GOING TO GRANDMA'S HOUSE FOR CHRISTMAS.
POOR PIPPI. WHAT ARE YOU GOING TO DO ON CHRISTMAS EVE ALL ALONE?
I'M GOING TO DANCE AROUND THE TREE WITH MY HORSE AND MR. NILSSON.
GOODBYE, DEAR, DEAR, PIPPI. MERRY CHRISTMAS!
TIDDLY-POM AND PIDDLY-DEE. THE WHOLE HOUSE WILL BE SNOWED IN WHEN YOU GET BACK.
WELL, IT LOOKS LIKE SOMEONE WANTS TO COME IN.
WOOF, WOOF!

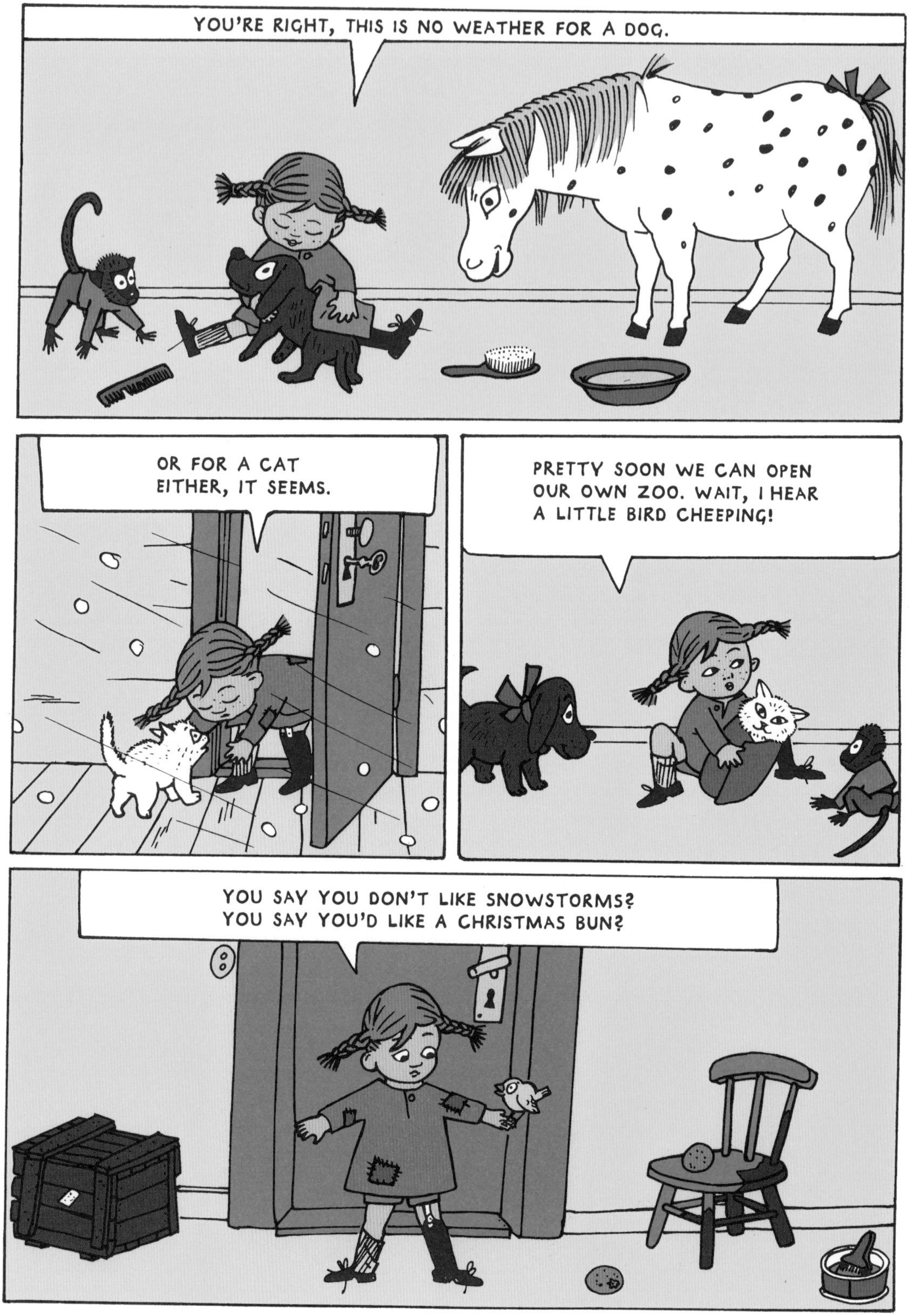
YOU'RE RIGHT, THIS IS NO WEATHER FOR A DOG.
OR FOR A CAT EITHER, IT SEEMS.
PRETTY SOON WE CAN OPEN OUR OWN ZOO. WAIT, I HEAR A LITTLE BIRD CHEEPING!
YOU SAY YOU DON'T LIKE SNOWSTORMS? YOU SAY YOU'D LIKE A CHRISTMAS BUN?

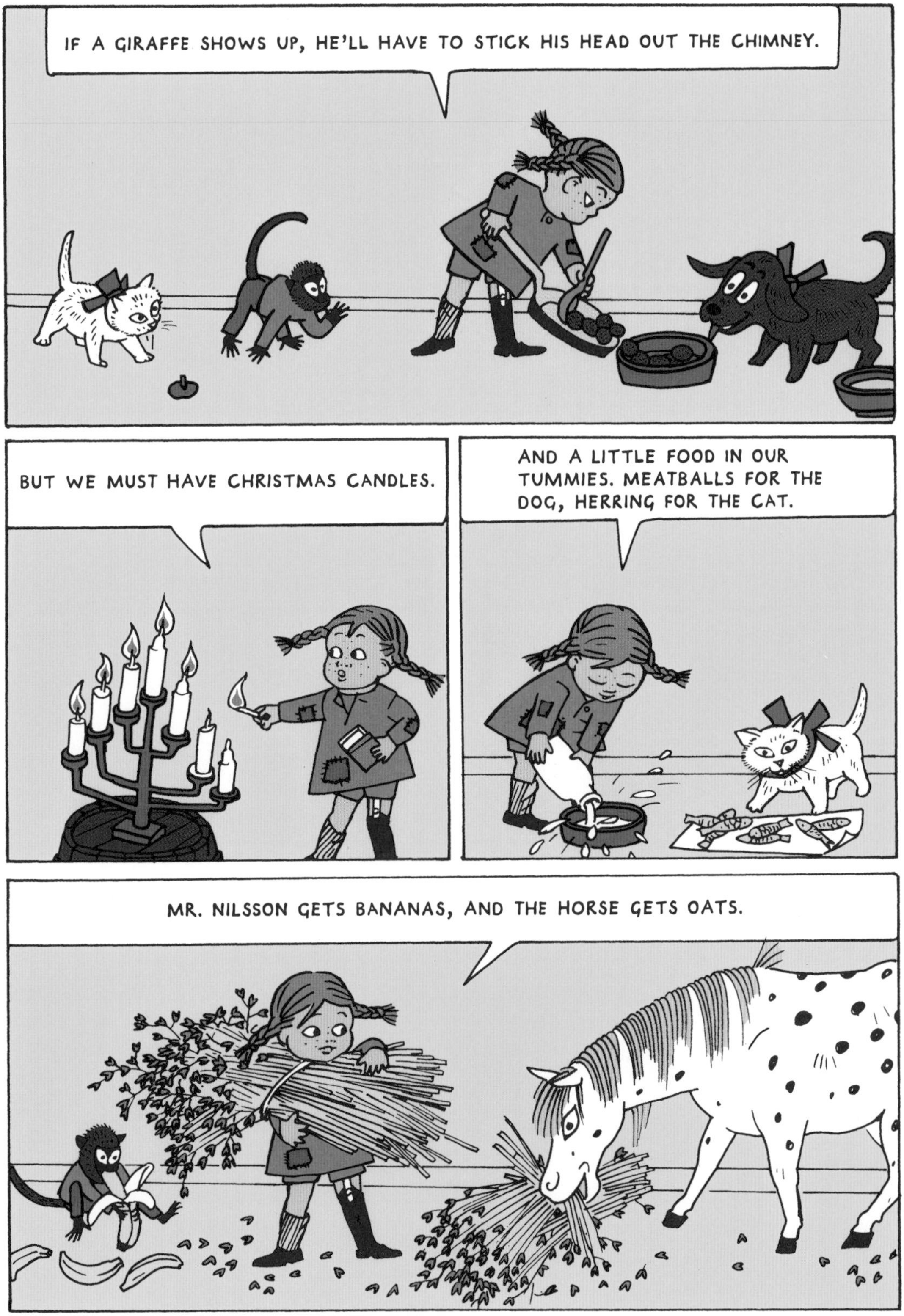
IF A GIRAFFE SHOWS UP, HE'LL HAVE TO STICK HIS HEAD OUT THE CHIMNEY.
BUT WE MUST HAVE CHRISTMAS CANDLES.
AND A LITTLE FOOD IN OUR TUMMIES. MEATBALLS FOR THE DOG, HERRING FOR THE CAT.
MR. NILSSON GETS BANANAS, AND THE HORSE GETS OATS.

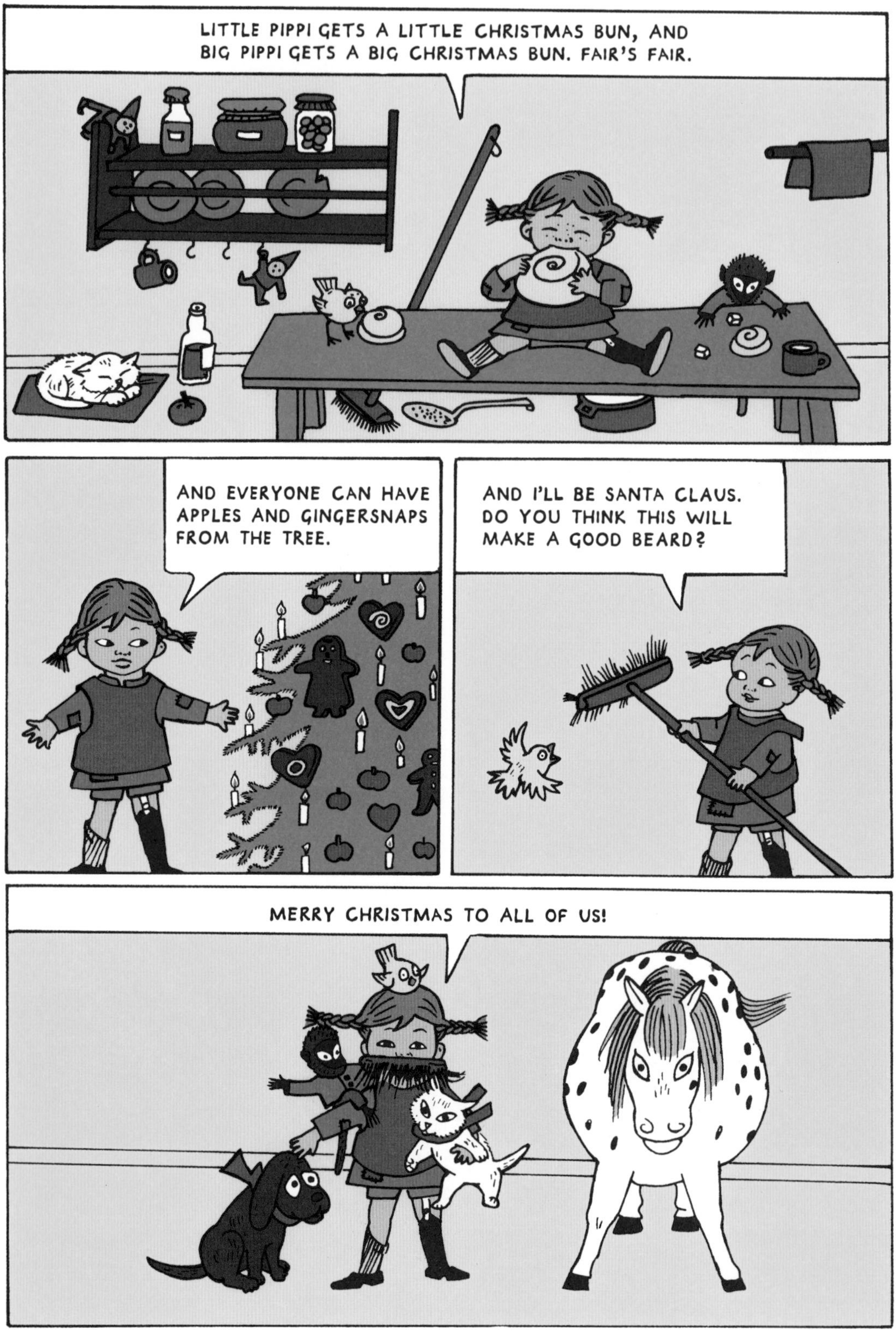
LITTLE PIPPI GETS A LITTLE CHRISTMAS BUN, AND BIG PIPPI GETS A BIG CHRISTMAS BUN. FAIR'S FAIR.
AND EVERYONE CAN HAVE APPLES AND GINGERSNAPS FROM THE TREE.
AND I'LL BE SANTA CLAUS. DO YOU THINK THIS WILL MAKE A GOOD BEARD?
MERRY CHRISTMAS TO ALL OF US!

Astrid Lindgren (1907–2002) was an immensely popular
children's book author as well as a lifelong philanthropist. Her Pippi Longstocking series–
Pippi Longstocking (1945), *Pippi Goes On Board* (1946), *Do You Know Pippi Longstocking?*
(1947), and *Pippi in the South Seas* (1948)–has been translated into more than sixty
languages and published all over the world.

During the winter of 1941, Lindgren's seven-year-old daughter Karin was ill, and asked her
mother to tell her a story about Pippi Longstocking. The story Astrid Lindgren told delighted
Karin and all her friends. A few years later, while recovering from an injury, Lindgren finally
found the time to write down the Pippi stories. Lindgren's tenth birthday present to her
daughter was the completed Pippi manuscript.

Lindgren submitted a revised version of the manuscript to the annual Rabén & Sjögren
writing contest, where it won first prize. The book was published in December of 1945, and
was an instant success. Rabén & Sjögren hired Lindgren as a children's book editor in 1946,
and she was soon put in charge of their children's book imprint, where she worked for many
years. Astrid Lindgren wrote more than seventy novels and storybooks, and has become
one of the world's best loved writers with over 145 million books sold worldwide.

Ingrid Vang Nyman (1916–1959) was a Danish-born
illustrator who was best known for her work on Swedish children's books. As a child, she
suffered from tuberculosis, and at age thirteen, she lost vision in one eye.

Vang Nyman studied at the Royal Danish Academy of Fine Arts in Copenhagen before
she moved to Stockholm, where her career in children's book illustration took off. She was
briefly married to the poet and painter Arne Nyman, with whom she had a son named Peder.
When the marriage ended in 1944, Ingrid Vang Nyman began a relationship with the lawyer
and author Uno Eng. It was also around this time that she created the first images of Pippi
Longstocking. The feisty Pippi was no doubt somewhat of a kindred spirit with Vang Nyman,
who had a strong faith in her own abilities, something not especially common among
children's book illustrators of the day. Ingrid Vang Nyman went on to illustrate numerous
children's books over the course of her brief career.

Tiina Nunnally is widely considered to be the preeminent translator
from Scandinavian languages into English. Her many awards and honors include the PEN/
BOMC Translation Prize for her work on Sigrid Undset's *Kristin Lavransdatter*. She grew up
in Milwaukee and received an M.A. in Scandinavian Studies from the University of Wisconsin.

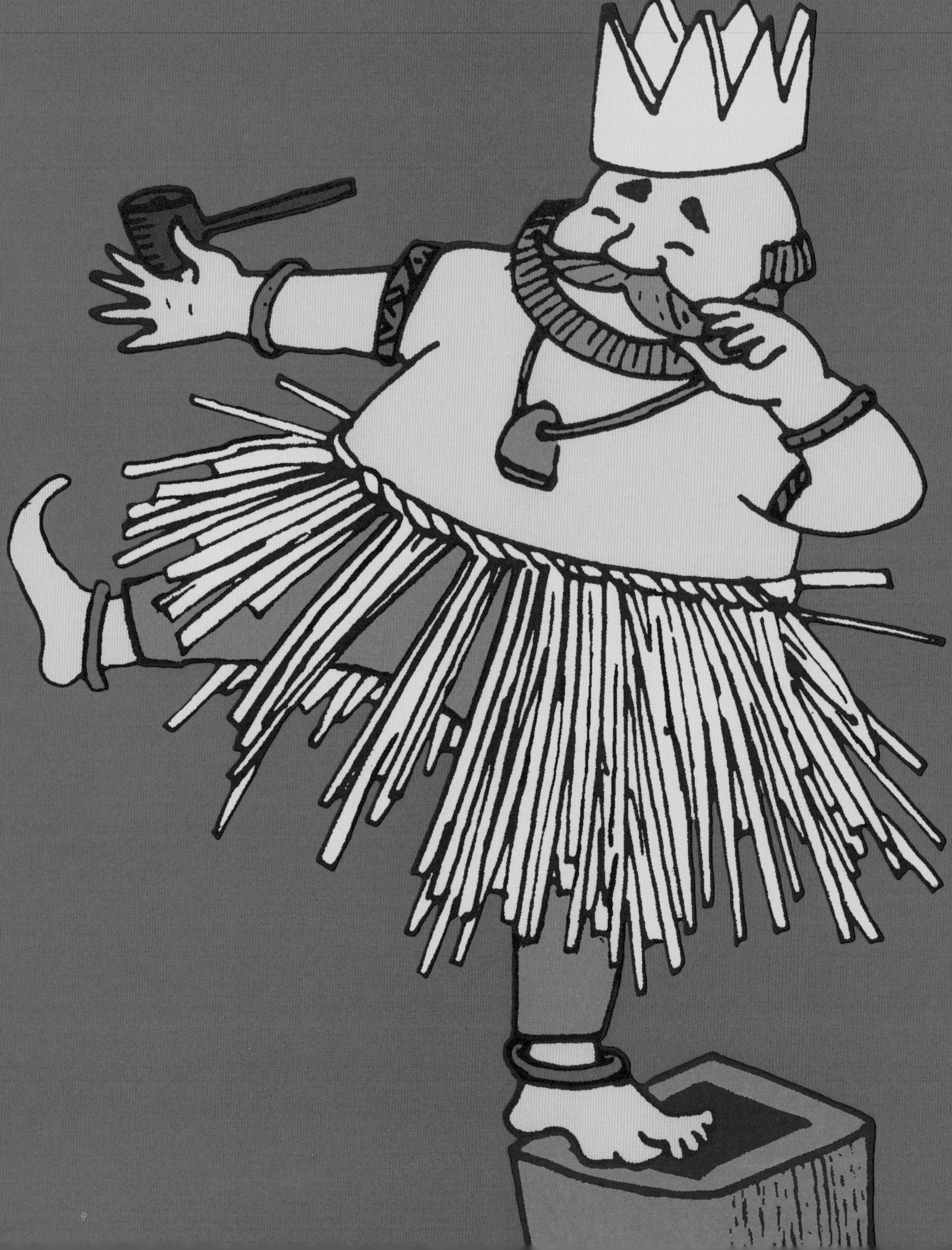

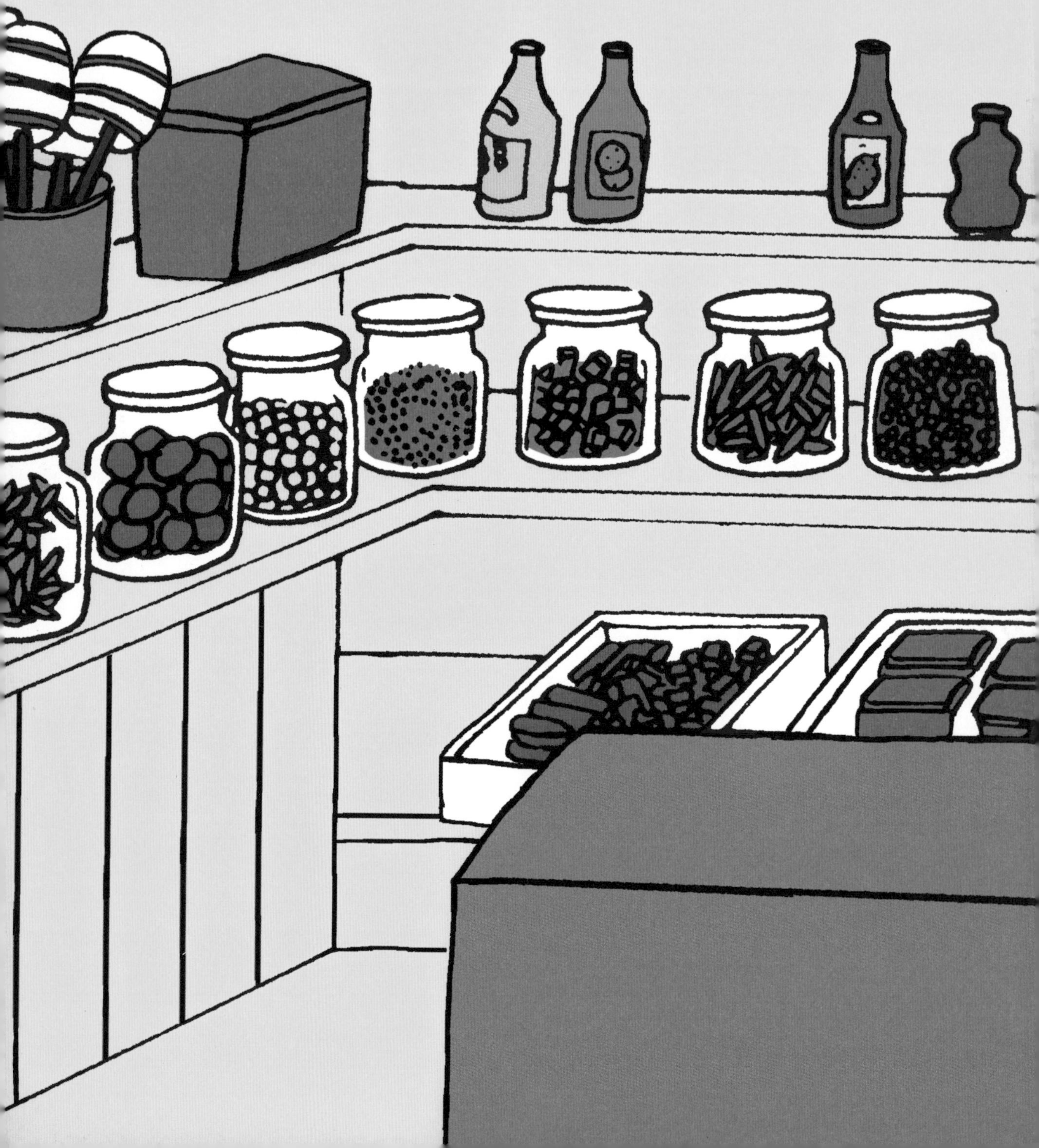

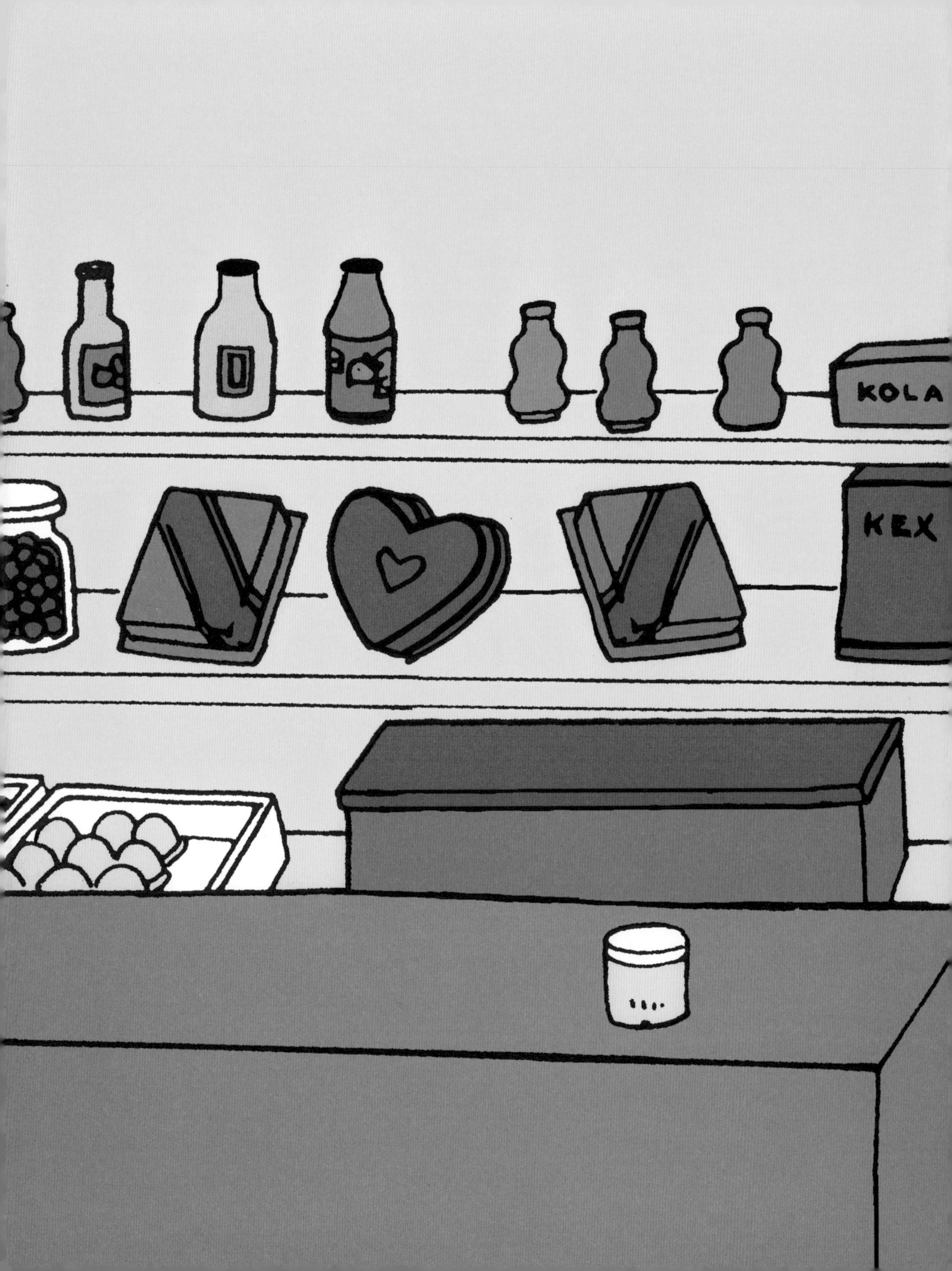
KOLA
KEX

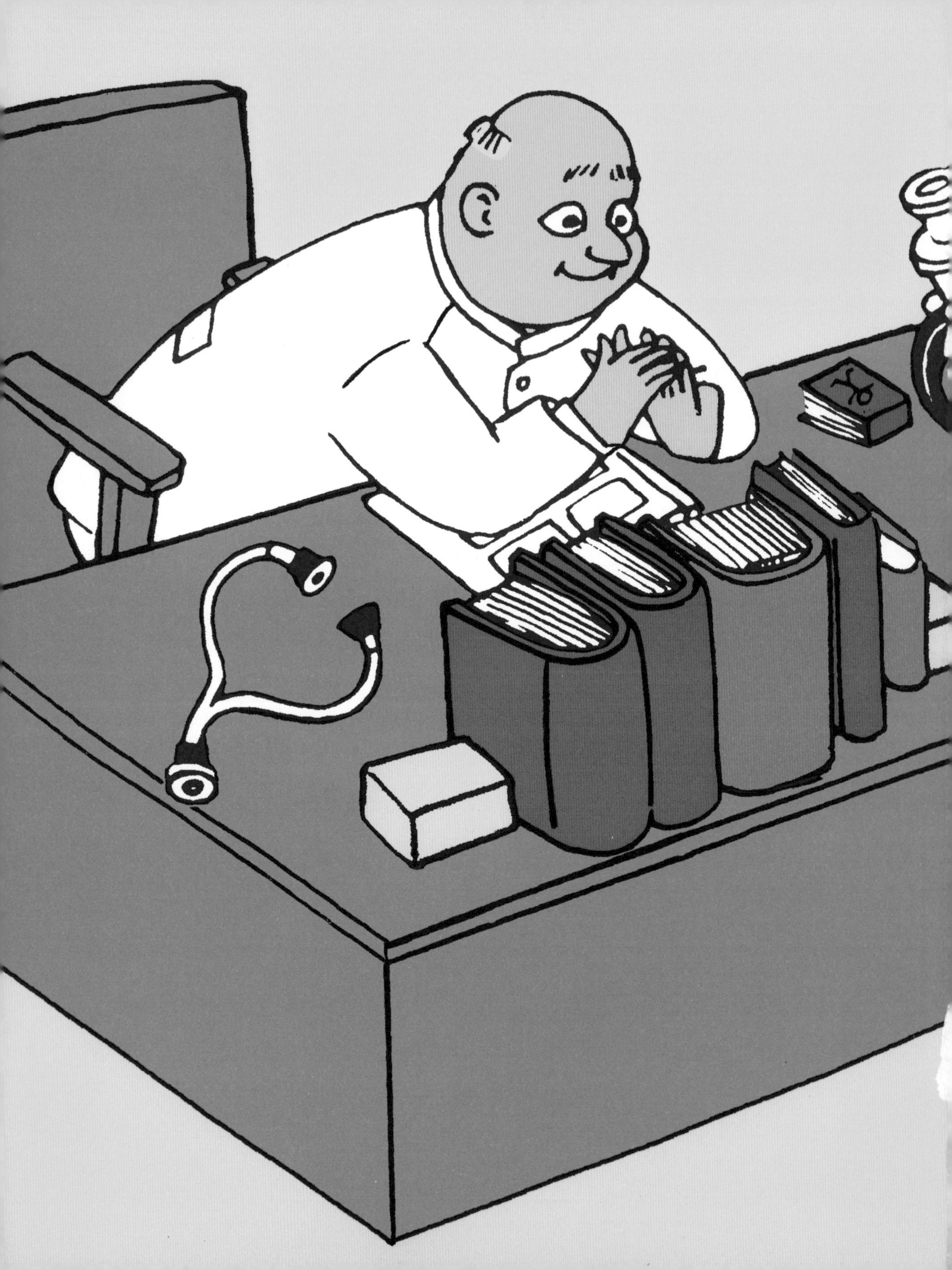

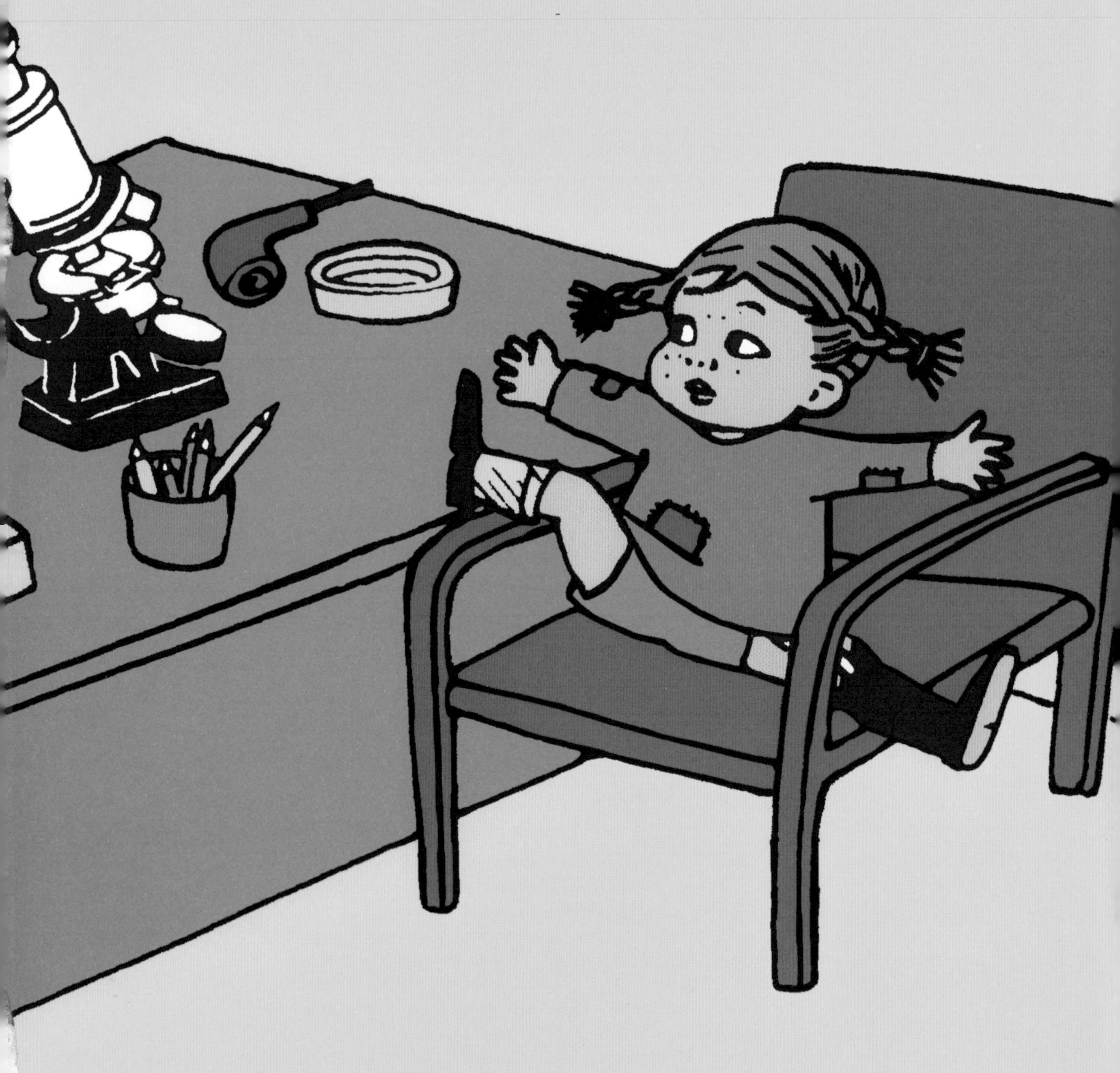

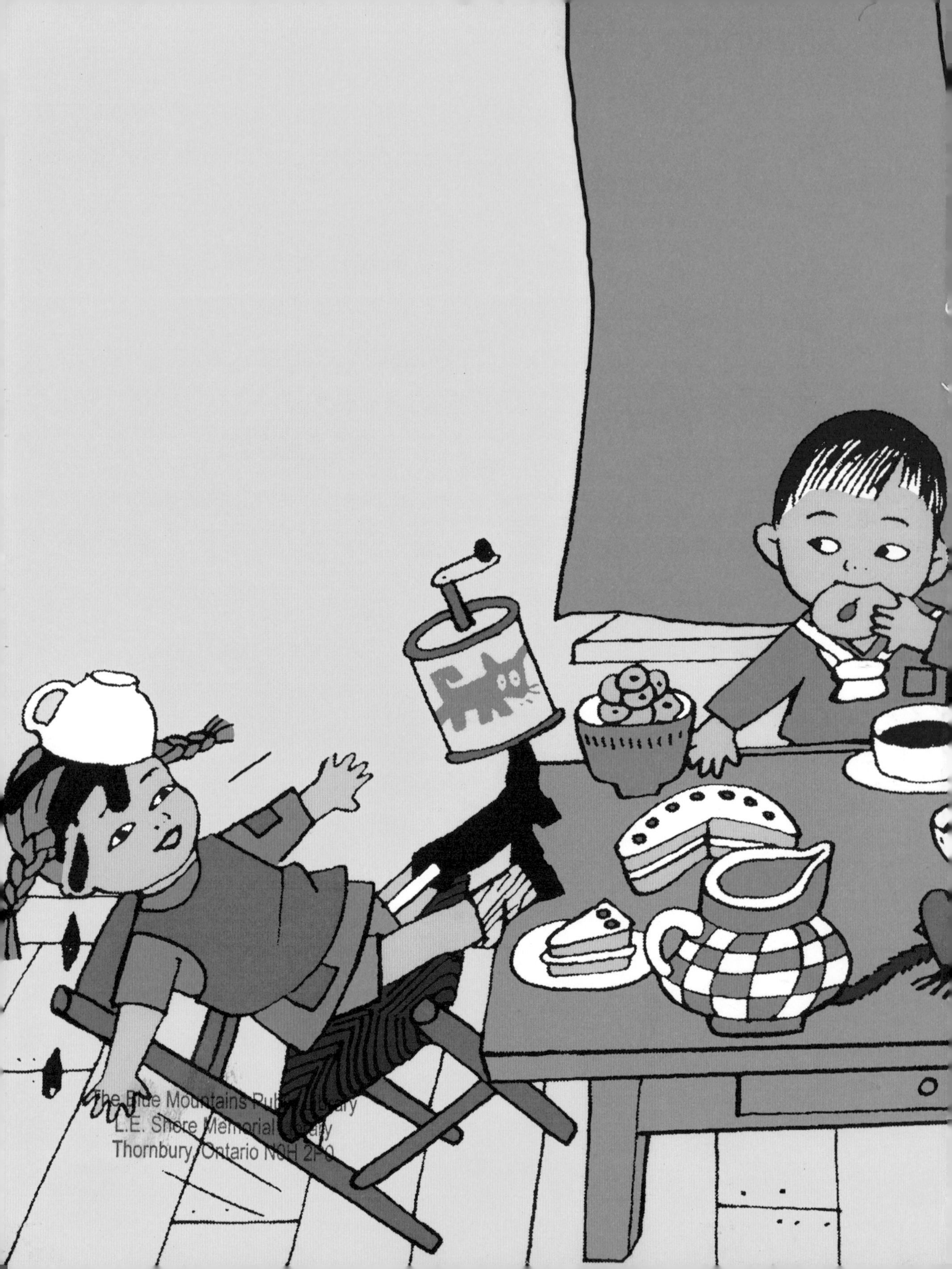